may
COOLER HEADS
prevail

may COOLER HEADS *prevail*

T. L. Dunnegan

ISBN 978-1-59789-676-4

Cover design: Faceout Studio, www.faceoutstudio.com

Published by Barbour Publishing, Inc., P.O. Box 719, Uhrichsville, Ohio 44683, www.barbourbooks.com

Our mission is to publish and distribute inspirational products offering exceptional value and biblical encouragement to the masses.

ecpa Member of the Evangelical Christian Publishers Association

Printed in the United States of America.

Dedication

We are all so thankful God allowed Teri to finish this book before taking her home. I know she was thankful, and she would have wanted to thank Faye Conn, Carol Davis and Diana Reed. Without their support and friendship, the struggle would have been uphill both ways in bare feet. We all miss her very much and can't wait to see her again.

—Patrick Dunnegan

CHAPTER ONE

In 1833, according to the Kenna Springs Historical Society, one of my ancestors, Tenacious Tanner, was accused of stealing Isaac Farley's horse. Unable to prove his innocence, Tenacious did the only thing he felt he could do. He broke out of jail and tracked down the real horse thief. Tenacious found the thief camped out by the Sapawhatchee River. But his attempt to take the man by surprise backfired. The horse thief suffered a heart attack and died. Tenacious, being tenacious, brought horse and corpse in tow back to Kenna Springs and insisted that the sheriff hang the dead man instead of him.

Ever since that infamous hanging, each succeeding generation of Tanners has been viewed by the townspeople of Kenna Springs as a generally God-fearing, but peculiar lot. And on the whole, the Tanner clan has always done their best to live up to the town's viewpoint.

Being a practical sort of child, I never considered myself the least bit peculiar and resented any action or behavior by any and all of my Tanner relatives, including my parents, that pointed in that direction. I was a lot more interested in sanity than most of my relatives. That being the case, eventually I earned a doctorate in clinical psychology. At age twenty-six I headed out into the world as Dr. Dixie J. Tanner.

I landed a very good position at a well-established clinic in Little Rock. With relatively good job security, insurance benefits, and a growing savings account, I felt like I had the world by the tail. Oddly enough, most of the Tanners thought I was the one acting peculiar. There's just no accounting for personal perception.

Six years ago, my parents, Jeb and Memphis Tanner, sold their farm in Kenna Springs and put a down payment on a little condo near the beach in Destin, Florida. It wasn't a huge surprise. We had vacationed in Destin as long as I could remember. Dad refers to the move to Destin as their "big adventure" in life. Mom calls it her dream retirement. The rest of the Tanners made bets on when they would come to their senses and move back to Kenna Springs.

Because my parents live in Florida, I now vacation there and only return to Kenna Springs for family reunions, family crisis situations, and the Kenna Springs Founder's Day festivities. This summer I managed to combine the Founder's Day festivities and a family crisis. I helped my fourth cousin, Dyson Tanner, and the potted plant that controls his mind, find a home in a very nice sanitarium.

Shortly thereafter, the Tanner clan divided up into two factions: those who argue that because Dyson's potted plant showed more sense than he ever did, I should have left well enough alone; and the second, which applauded my efforts and have looked upon me as a one-woman free mental health clinic ever since.

Tanners seldom let much time go by between one family crisis and another. Still, I was surprised when, after brushing off a nightmare blind date early in the evening and settling down in my comfy pajamas with a late night bowl of cereal, the phone rang and it was Uncle Rudd.

By the clock on my kitchen wall, it was eleven thirty when I said hello.

Uncle Rudd, from the free mental health clinic side of the family, firmly announced, "Dixie-gal, glad I caught you. Tried a little earlier, but you weren't home. We got a family problem up here, and we need your help. You'll need to make arrangements to stay a few days, so you go ahead and get things rolling, and I'll fill you in when you get here. We'll be expecting you soon."

He hung up, and I was left standing in my kitchen with a bowl of soggy cereal in one hand and a dead phone in the other. Feeling stunned, and wondering what the Tanners had gotten themselves into this time, I put the bowl of cereal on the counter and punched in Uncle Rudd's phone number.

Before he had a chance to say anything but hello, I jumped in. "Not so fast. I'm tired, it's late, and it will certainly not be easy for me to make arrangements to get a few days off. Bottom line, I'm not going anywhere until you tell me what's going on."

"Dixie-gal, you just gotta trust me on this. We need you, or I wouldn't have called. I'll tell you what's going on when you get here."

I asked the only question that made sense. "Has someone in the family passed away?"

I heard Uncle Rudd sputter the words "family" and "passed away" like they were foreign concepts to him. Then he bellowed so loud I had to hold the phone away from my ear. "Well, I wouldn't call that little ferret-faced varmint, Aaron Scott, family, but he's dead just the same!"

Even with my uncle's rather colorful description, I couldn't dredge up a mental picture of this Aaron Scott. Finally, I gave up. "Do I know this man?"

"Not exactly," he admitted. "Connie didn't cotton to talkin' about the man very much, so naturally the rest of us didn't, either. The Scott family live around Brogan's Ferry. Aaron Scott, in particular, is the scummy little toad that skipped town and left your Aunt Connie standing at the altar on their wedding day over forty years ago."

I knew that someone had left Aunt Connie at the altar, and as a result she had never married, but I had never heard anyone speak his name. As far as I knew it was one of the best kept secrets, if not the only secret, in Kenna Springs.

"And you want me to attend his funeral?" I obviously didn't get the point.

"Dixie-gal," Uncle Rudd groaned, "Aaron didn't just pass

away in his sleep real peaceful like. He was murdered."

Murdered! The word slammed around in my head from one side to the other, giving me the beginnings of a terrific headache.

"And it wasn't my baby sister that done him in, if that's what you're thinkin'," he growled. "But it sure looks like she did!"

Right then and there I should have hung up the phone, packed my bags, and moved into a condo near my parents. Instead, I asked the question I wasn't sure I wanted the answer to. "Okay, Uncle Rudd, why does it look like Aunt Connie murdered this guy?"

Uncle Rudd huffed. "It's against my better judgment, but I'll give you the bare bones of it. None of us has seen or heard from Aaron Scott since he left Connie at the altar. That is, until he showed up here in town sometime yesterday evening. Nissa and I heard about it when we were having supper over at Patsy's Café tonight. 'Course, we got worried about how Connie was going to react, so we drove over to her place. We parked in the alley behind the flower shop, like we always do. We started to head up the stairs to her place over the shop when we noticed the back door to the shop was cracked open some and the lights were on inside. Nissa thought maybe Connie was so flustered at hearing that Aaron Scott was back in town that she forgot to turn off the lights and shut the door when she closed up the flower shop for the evening. We went in. . .and, well. . .that's. . ."

Uncle Rudd's voice trailed off until he stopped talking. I waited quietly. Finally, I heard him take a deep breath and let it out. "That's when we found Connie and Aaron in the shop. Connie was sitting on the floor, moaning, and her eyes were all crazy-like. We tried to get her to talk to us, but she started saying stuff that didn't make a whole lot of sense. She just moaned and rocked back and forth holding Scott in her arms, and him just laying there with a pair of her flower-cutting scissors sticking out of his back."

Uncle Rudd's voice quivered, and he quit talking. I knew I should respond, but I couldn't translate my thoughts into words.

My head began to throb in earnest. Somewhere in the back of my mind was the perfectly good notion that I needed to move someplace where there are no telephones and no one could even pronounce the name Tanner.

I had heard enough to know this didn't look good for Aunt Connie. I started to speak, but my mouth was so dry I had to stop and clear my throat. Swallowing as best I could, I croaked out the words, "Would you mind telling me again why you think Aunt Connie didn't kill this Aaron Scott? I must have missed it the first time around."

"Now see here, young lady," Uncle Rudd bellowed again. "You just proved my point. You think she killed him, just like everyone else around Kenna Springs will. But I got her to make just enough sense to know that she didn't kill him. I know good and well it looks bad for Connie. That's why it's up to us Tanners to prove she didn't do it." Uncle Rudd paused for a brief second, then announced, "And I've come up with a plan to do just that!"

I immediately quit worrying about my aching head and my cotton-spitting mouth and felt the *thump*, *thump* of a nervous tic that was developing at the corner of my left eye. All things considered, I didn't care that my voice sounded a bit testy when I asked, "Plan? What plan?"

"I ain't got all the particulars worked out yet on how we're gonna catch that killer. That's why we need you up here."

"You want me to help you work out the particulars on a plan to catch a killer?" I couldn't keep the shrillness out of my voice. "Uncle Rudd, that's just. . .well it's just. . ." I wanted to use the word "insane." Instead I settled for, "It's just not practical."

"I'll work out the plan, Dixie-gal, you don't need to worry about that. We need you for something else. See, Connie is pretty rattled, and she keeps talking in some kinda code. Nissa calls it symbols. Don't matter what you want to call it, we can't make heads or tails of it. So I was thinking that since you did such a good job with cousin Dyson, and you know all that psycho mumbo jumbo, you could help us decipher what Connie is talking about. Then we would have our first clue as to who really killed Aaron Scott."

"It's psychological mumbo jumbo, if you please," I muttered, wondering how I could explain to my uncle that this was a lot different than finding Dyson a nice place in which to be psychotic. I'm not trained to decipher coded messages—or find murder clues for that matter.

I knew Uncle Rudd wouldn't listen for two seconds to all the sane reasons I shouldn't get mixed up in this mess, so I settled for what I considered to be the next best tactic and said, "Of course, I'll be there to support Aunt Connie in any way I can. But Sheriff Otis may want a therapist that is licensed in the state of Missouri to talk with her."

"Doesn't matter what the sheriff wants," he huffed, "because tellin' Otis Beecher isn't part of the plan."

Fearing that Uncle Rudd had, as so many Tanners before him, excused himself from the Dinner Table of Intelligent Reasoning, and was now in a feeding frenzy at the Buffet for the Befuddled, I used the same calm, well-modulated voice I had used with Dyson. "Maybe it would be a good idea to inform Otis about Aaron Scott's murder. After all, Otis is the sheriff as well as a friend of the family. I'm certain he'll see to it that the truth comes out. Besides, one cannot simply leave dead bodies lying about and expect people not to notice. Surely this man's family is wondering what happened to him?"

"Nope, nobody will be missing him," Uncle Rudd replied gruffly, "because nobody knows he's dead. We hid the body where no one will find it."

I knew it! The minute Uncle Rudd used the word *problem*, I should have packed my bags, bypassed Florida, and headed out for some remote South Sea island where I could learn to juggle coconuts and simultaneously sing "Nobody Knows the Trouble I've Seen." But since it was now the middle of the night and much too late to get in touch with a travel agent, I pleaded, "Be reasonable, Uncle Rudd. Where in Kenna Springs could you possibly hide a dead body? It's a small town. People see things, people know things."

"Reasonable?" Uncle Rudd exploded. "You want me to be reasonable? If old Tenacious Tanner had been reasonable, they'da hung him for horse stealin' instead of that dead horse thief. I'm telling you straight out, we hid that body real good. Nobody is gonna find it unless we want 'em to. End of story!"

"All right, all right, you don't have to yell," I told him. "But you and Aunt Nissa locked up in jail for hiding a dead body is not how I want either one of you spending your golden years."

"What? You think I'd let Nissa drag around a dead man? I'm not that big a clod. She took Connie upstairs, got her some things packed up, and then took her out to the car while we did what we had to do."

Since the "we" part wasn't Aunt Nissa, I was left to wonder which cousin was egging on this latest Tanner madness. Personally, my vote would've gone to cousin Woody. At one time there was talk of reinstating hanging in Kenna Springs just for the benefit of seeing Woody swing. However, no one had seen or heard from Woody since he took off for California ten years ago, and Woody's parents moved to Florida soon after. It couldn't be cousin Dyson and his potted plant. I had talked to Dyson on the phone this morning (I declined the opportunity to chat with the plant). No one else came flashing into my mind, so I asked, "Who is 'we' then?"

"We've talked long enough, Dixie-gal. It's time you started packing. I'll tell you the rest when you get up here." Uncle Rudd hung up.

He had me and he knew it. As things stood, there was a murderer running loose in my hometown, a dead body tucked away from prying eyes, an aunt who apparently now speaks in code, and a sheriff who knew nothing about any of it. And of course, the Tanner family was right in the thick of things. What choice did I have? I packed my bags.

CHAPTER TWO

It was a little after one o'clock in the morning by the time I got on the road. I was still fretting and stewing over Uncle Rudd's crazy announcement that he and an unknown sidekick had hidden the body of a murdered man and were going after his killer. It was insane at best, dangerous at worst.

I didn't know what or how much of all of this to tell my secretary, Estelle Biggs, so I decided it would be best for everyone concerned if I just waited until I sorted it out in my mind before I called her. Besides, Estelle is not the kind of person one wakes up in the middle of the night. She has always been quite clear on that point. Considering that I was about to put her through rearranging my schedule and finding someone to take my case load for a few days, maybe longer, it was best to wait until I knew she was awake. I figured I could call her about the time I made it to the city limits of Kenna Springs. Right now I had enough worries and woes to think about with Uncle Rudd playing hide-and-seek with dead men and murderers.

Traffic was almost nonexistent, and I had nearly six hours

of driving time ahead. With that in mind, I tried to focus on what I could say to persuade Uncle Rudd to give up on this harebrained idea of playing detective and call Sheriff Otis. I came up with nothing, nada, zip. It was frustrating. The more frustrated I got, the more my favorite childhood daydream kept intruding into my thoughts. I had forgotten about it for years, yet there it was, as fresh and inviting as the first day I dreamed it up. I tried to think about something else, anything else. It was just a silly daydream about the way I wanted things to be. Maybe it was because I was tired, maybe it was just the frustration, or both, but finally I gave in to the comforting reverie.

I had it all worked out by the time I was eight years old. In my daydream I was adopted. My real parents were poor, but sane people, who had come on hard times and couldn't afford to take care of me the way they wanted to. One day while looking for work, they happened by a nice-looking farmhouse belonging to Jeb and Memphis Tanner. Being from Chicago, they knew nothing about the Tanners, and so they were unaware of the various Tanner quirks that get passed down from generation to generation. Wanting me to have what they couldn't give me at the time, they reluctantly left me, a newborn baby wrapped in a threadbare blanket, on the farmhouse steps. Heartbroken, they went in search of work, thinking someday they would come back for me. That evening they were caught outside of town in a blinding blizzard. Holding each other close, slowly freezing to death, they proclaimed their undying love for each other and their darling baby daughter, and breathed their last.

I cherished that daydream, until one day, in a fit of childish petulance, I announced to my mother that I knew good and well I was adopted and told her the story I had come to hope was true. It didn't take my bewildered mother long to produce my birth certificate, which of course had the names of Jeb and Memphis Tanner as the proud parents of one daughter, Dixie June Tanner, typed on it. My mother also pointed out that I was born in June and there was not a snowflake in sight at the time. Then she remarked that I had her small frame and dark hair. And just in case I had any lingering doubts, she snatched a color photo of my dad off the mantle of the living room fireplace and led me over to a mirror. Holding the picture up next to my face she said, "Honey, you look like me in the face, but you have the Tanner eyes."

I couldn't deny the truth of that. I do have the Tanner eyes. Not all the Tanners are born with them, but there are enough of us to make it a family trait. And I had them. One eye is greenish-brown and the other is just brown. Oh, how I have pined for baby blues. Even though my vision is 20/20, I tried colored contacts once, but threw them away after the redness and swelling started. So, I am a Tanner. I admit it, but not without many, many reservations.

Crossing the Missouri state line, I didn't have time to think about anything but my driving. My old, but much loved, CJ-7 Jeep started slowing down to a crawl on the hills, even though I pressed the gas pedal all the way to the floorboard. There was no place open to get it checked out.

By the time I reached Shotgun Hill, just outside of Kenna Springs, I had lost a lot of time. I rounded the bend at the top of the hill and came out onto a straight patch of road. It was already past eight o'clock. Estelle would be up and getting ready for church by now. The weather was clear enough and the road wide enough, I could pull over and make the phone call.

I pressed her number on my speed dial. She answered on the third ring. No, it wouldn't be easy to rearrange my schedule on such short notice, but since I had some sort of family emergency that I refused to specify, she would manage. I thanked her and hung up. I felt guilty about not telling her any details, but what else could I do? I didn't want to lie, and I sure didn't want to tell her why I was going to Kenna Springs.

As I rounded the second bend before starting down Shotgun Hill, I had a panoramic view of Kenna Springs. It is one of those quaint old towns made up of stone, wood, and brick. Since it's close to a network of natural springs and a fair-sized lake, Kenna Springs has always been a minor tourist attraction. During the summer months the tourists spend just enough money in the antique shops and craft stores dotted around the square to keep everyone hopeful that next year will be even better.

I loved Kenna Springs as it looked now, dressed to the

nines in an array of fall colors. The tourists have gone home, and everything and everyone moves to a slower cadence.

At the bottom of Shotgun Hill sits Jobina's Jellies and Jams canning factory. Jobina's Jellies and Jams is the biggest employer in the county. It was originally founded by Eldon and Jobina Sheffield. Their grandson, Latham, runs the factory now, making him the wealthiest man in several counties.

As I drove around the town square, I noticed that Truman Spencer, the owner/editor of the Kenna Springs *Bugle*, was leaving the newspaper office with a small box in one hand and a clip-on tie in the other. Next door to the newspaper, Ed Baringer, dressed in his Sunday suit, was taping a sign up on his storefront window advertising the community-wide bake sale at the Veteran's Hall next week. Even Maybelle Chesewick was out and about, pushing her battered grocery cart, which was already half-full of whatever odds and ends she happened to find lying around.

I couldn't help but slow down as I drove past Aunt Connie's Red Carnations Flower Shop. The shop was dark except for the lights in the display windows on each side of the front entrance.

Turning north off the square, I passed the older part of town with its two-story Victorian homes, decked out in colorful gingerbread trim. Once past the residential area, I headed out on the country road toward Uncle Rudd and Aunt Nissa's farm, then turned into the half-mile driveway that led up to the two-story white farmhouse.

As I drove up and parked by the garage, I could see Aunt Nissa waiting in her rocker on the front porch. Smiling and waving a greeting, she started walking toward the Jeep.

"My goodness, child, we thought you would be here before now," she said, reaching out to hug me.

"I'm sorry. I would've been here sooner, but something's wrong with my Jeep," I explained. "I'm just grateful it didn't quit on me. I thought about calling, but I thought you might be trying to get some sleep."

"Well, you're here now. Rudd'll take a look at the Jeep. In the meantime, you just come on inside and let me get you some breakfast." Eyeing me up and down, she sighed. "You're like your mama, a little on the puny side, but I'll do what I can while you're here."

"Breakfast does sound pretty good about now." I grinned at her. Aunt Nissa is a firm believer in feeding anyone who crosses the threshold of her home. Fortunately she is one of the best cooks in the county.

Stowing my bags by the staircase, we went on into the kitchen. The smell of fresh-baked biscuits and bacon permeated Aunt Nissa's cheery red and white kitchen.

I took what I have always considered as my seat at the table. "Are Uncle Rudd and Aunt Connie still asleep?"

"Connie is still asleep. We gave her a sleeping pill. Rudd is out doing some chores, but he'll be in directly." Aunt Nissa piled scrambled eggs, bacon, and hash browns, along with a biscuit loaded with gravy onto a plate. She handed me the plate then poured a glass of milk and set it on the table.

"Are you going to go to church with us this morning?" she asked, pouring herself a glass of milk and sitting down at the table across from me.

Although I have a church home that I love and cherish in Little Rock, the little nondenominational church most of my family belongs to in Kenna Springs has always held a special place in my heart. I grew up in that church. I was loved and cared for there. It was there I learned my first Bible verses, learned that Jesus is alive and well and what He does for the living. A part of me wanted to go to church, but my eyes were burning from lack of sleep. Mostly I just wanted to finish breakfast and climb into one of Aunt Nissa's beds.

Swallowing a bite of crisp bacon, I shook my head. "Not this time. I'm pretty tired, and as much as I love Pastor Jeff's preaching, I don't think I could stay awake this morning while he's encouraging the flock."

"Of course, dear." Aunt Nissa gave me a little nod. "You just finish up with your breakfast, and we'll take your bags on upstairs and get you settled in. I've already freshened up the lilac room for you. You can talk to Rudd and Connie after a nap."

I had just enough energy and curiosity to ask, "Do you really think it's a good idea for Uncle Rudd to go after whoever murdered this Aaron Scott fellow by himself?"

Aunt Nissa pondered the question just long enough for

me to be hopeful before she said, "Well. . .Rudd promised he would be careful. And I really don't see any other way, dear."

Aunt Nissa has obviously been a Tanner a tad too long.

"But there is another way," I wailed. "You can call Sheriff Otis and let him find the person who murdered Aaron Scott. Don't you think that would be a lot less dangerous?"

"Oh no, dear, we really couldn't do that," Aunt Nissa said, shaking her head so hard she nearly jiggled the bun on top of her head out of place. "You really must understand the situation, dear. Connie can't remember much of anything about last night. Rudd is afraid Otis wouldn't have any other choice but to arrest her. I know it would be less dangerous to call Otis and let him handle it, but you can see, can't you, there isn't any other course of action open to us."

I suddenly felt like the woman who shows up late at a clearance sale. I simply didn't stand a chance. So for the time being, I pushed aside my plate and gave in. "Okay, we'll talk about it after I get some sleep."

As we negotiated the staircase with my luggage in tow, I came to a decision. The best way for me to help all three of them was to borrow one of Uncle Rudd's vehicles and head back to Little Rock first thing in the morning to cash in my one and only certificate of deposit, along with my small, but growing, stash of money in a mutual fund. Because, bless them, they were going to need all the bail money they could get.

Aunt Nissa and I unloaded my bags next to the four-poster bed in what she refers to as the lilac room. It has always been a peculiarity of hers to refer to rooms by color.

"Dixie dear, I was thinking that while you're getting settled maybe it would be good for us to chat about something else besides this horrible murder. I think you would sleep better if we sort of take our minds off our troubles for just a bit before you take a nap."

"Sure. What would you like to talk about?" I wasn't actually in the mood to be talking about anything. All I wanted was sleep. But an aunt is an aunt, and I have always had a soft spot in my heart for Aunt Nissa, so I figured it wouldn't hurt to chat for a few minutes.

She sat down, making herself quite comfortable in the white wicker rocker near the bed. Then, smiling shyly at me, she opened with, "You know, dear, since Rudd and I were never blessed with children, we consider you the closest we can come to having a daughter. So, let's catch up a little with what's going on in your life. Have you seen any good movies, eaten at any interesting places, been dating anyone special?" Then, with all the subtlety of a fox in a hen house, she patted her pearly white hair. "Rudd called a time or two before he got ahold of you. I thought maybe you were out on a date with some nice young man."

Only Aunt Nissa would consider a date more important than a murder. The woman is truly obsessed with my love life, or lack thereof. Over the past three or four years, it has been of grave concern to Aunt Nissa that I am not married. Every summer when I come up to help her with the preparations for the big fish fry on Founder's Day, she takes it upon herself to introduce me to every available bachelor she can find within a three-county radius. I've come to look upon that time of year as the Kenna Springs Founder's Day Fish Fry and Dixie Tanner Manhunt.

As I stood there contemplating my answer, I knew I could lie. That would be the easy way out. But lies always seem to catch up with me somehow, so I braced myself and told the truth. "Yes, I happened to be on a date last night. It was one of those blind dates that didn't turn out well at all. So, no, there is no one special in my life."

"Now, how do you know this young man isn't your special someone, dear?" Aunt Nissa asked. "You've only had one date with him."

"Trust me, the man I went out with last night is not my special someone."

"Well, no one is perfect, dear. I'm sure if you really looked, you might find some good qualities about this man. You're thirty-three years old, honey, maybe you should be thinking about settling down."

I glared at her as much as one can glare at a much-loved, but determined aunt, and said, "The particular man I had a date with last night seems to think that a two-thousand-year-old Babylonian undertaker speaks through him. And as far as I could tell, neither one of them could sit upright and chew meat at the same time. And just for the record, I am thirty-two. . .at least until next June."

"My, you do need a nap, dear." Aunt Nissa jumped up and bustled around the room. "I'll just turn down your sheets and go on downstairs to get things cleaned up before church."

Once she left the room, I cracked the window open. The cool air smelled fresh and clean. There's something invigorating about the wind in the fall. Tired as I was at the moment, I pulled the wicker rocker up to the open window and sat breathing in the fresh air and watching the leaves on the ground as they danced their last dance. I started to nod off in the chair and decided it was time for me to get some sleep.

I took off my tennis shoes and crawled under the covers, not caring that I was still dressed in my sweatsuit. My last thought was that I was sorry I had snapped at Aunt Nissa.

CHAPTER THREE

As I woke, I felt, rather than saw someone in the room with me. I heard a *clickity-click-clickity-click-clickity-click* noise, so I pried one eye open to see what was making such an irritating sound.

The clicking came from the knitting needles Aunt Connie was using. She had pulled the wicker rocker right next to the bed and rocked and knitted with what looked to me like the speed of light. The fruit of her labors seemed to be a long blue thing piling up on her lap.

Eyeing me over the top of her knitting, she said, "'Bout time you woke up. Thought maybe you got it into your head you're some sort of sleeping beauty. Guess you've never seen yourself sleep."

Aunt Connie literally cackled at her own joke. She even slapped her knee, apparently not noticing she was the only one laughing.

I did my very best impression of a person waking up from a sound sleep and mumbled, "What time is it?"

She shrugged and kept on knitting. "Don't know. I suppose since you're awake, it's time to get up."

"I see. Well, in that case I'd better get my shoes on."

It occurred to me, while I was scrounging for my left tennis shoe underneath the bed, that Aunt Connie was certainly her usual mouthy self and seemed in peak form.

"You always sleep in your clothes like that?" she asked.

"It's a failing of mine. Anytime I go more than twenty-four hours without sleep, I tend to crash wherever and however I can."

"That so?" Aunt Connie stuffed her knitting into a red paisley bag and stood up. "Rudd and Nissa got back from church awhile ago. I'm gonna go on down and help set out lunch. You come on when you've a mind to."

She stopped at the doorway, turned, and gave me a long look. "I reckon Rudd called you about last night."

I nodded my head.

"You know then that Rudd's set on finding out who murdered my Aaron. Which means the only man I ever loved is dead, and I have an idiot for a brother. I agreed to go along with this business last night 'cause I was half out of my head with grief." Aunt Connie heaved a mournful sigh then added, "Today things look a bit different. I'm gonna talk Rudd outta this fool notion, so you keep them bags packed, Dixie June. You just might be goin' home sooner than you think."

She shut the door so fast I didn't have time to tell her that

I wholeheartedly agreed with her.

Cheerfully leaving my bags packed, I grabbed my makeup bag and sprinted down the hall to the bathroom to clean up a little before we ate.

By the time I made it downstairs, lunch was already on the table. Before I could sit down, I received a bear hug from Uncle Rudd. "Dixie-gal, good to see you." His voice boomed in my ear. Once everyone was at the table, we bowed our heads while Uncle Rudd, a firm believer in chatting often and long with the Almighty, took his time saying grace.

While we were all filling our plates, it hit me that over the years Uncle Rudd had somehow grown older. When had that happened and why hadn't I noticed it? He had always been a big man, and hard work kept his muscles from turning to flab. But I couldn't remember when he had added those extra pounds, or when his salt-and-pepper hair had lost most of the pepper. Uncle Rudd could be exasperating at times, but he's a good-hearted man, and I love him. Right now, I was afraid for him—for all of us really. A shiver went down my spine, and I desperately hoped that when the time came, he would listen to Aunt Connie.

Other than comments like "Please pass the rolls," and, "Pastor Jeff preached a great sermon this morning," we were a pretty quiet bunch at the kitchen table. By silent, unanimous agreement, none of us spoke about the murder while we were eating.

Once lunch was over and the dishes done, it was time for

a family discussion. Aunt Connie and I put away our dish towels and took our seats. Aunt Nissa poured coffee, while Uncle Rudd went into the other room and came back with a file folder, legal pad, and pen.

"We want to do this thing real organized and official-like," he commented as he sat down.

"I got something I want to say to you, Rudd," Aunt Connie ventured.

Holding up a hand for silence, Uncle Rudd said, "Wait a minute, Connie, then you can say your piece, okay?" Not waiting for a yea or nay from his sister, Uncle Rudd cleared his throat and continued, "I know this is gonna be tough for you to talk about, but if we don't nab whoever murdered Aaron, the only one they'll point to is you, Little Sis. If that happens, you'd have to sell your shop just to pay the legal fees. Of course, we'd all chip in what we could, but I don't think even a good lawyer could keep you outta jail." He crossed his arms on the table and leaned toward Aunt Connie. His eyes worried and soft, he spoke to her in a hushed voice. "It near breaks my heart to think about you livin' out your days huddled up, all lonely-like, on a narrow bunk, in a six-by-ten, skanky-smelling jail cell. So, you can see why we can't go to Sheriff Otis about this, don't you, Sis?"

Pale-faced and wide-eyed, Aunt Connie slowly nodded her head. That wasn't exactly the go-get-'em attitude I was hoping for.

Uncle Rudd reached over to pat her hand and asked,

"Now, what was it you wanted to say, Sis?"

"Thank you," she squeaked.

"Oh now, you don't have to thank me." Uncle Rudd beamed. "We're Tanners, you know, and Tanners take care of each other."

I was disappointed that Aunt Connie was not going to talk Uncle Rudd out of this wild caper, but after listening to Uncle Rudd talk about smelly jail cells, I understood her change of heart. That left me with the question of whether or not Uncle Rudd had called my parents.

When I asked, Uncle Rudd turned to look at me, smiling that big lopsided smile of his. "Well now, Dixie-gal, I sure did think about it. But I decided there wasn't much they could do. Besides, by the time they drive all the way from Florida, we'll have everything wrapped up all nice and neat-like. It's nice of you to want them in on things, though."

In on things! I had lived all my life in abject fear that my parents would be "in on things." I was so relieved that Uncle Rudd wasn't going to call them that I smiled back at him. "Well, if you think that's best."

He nodded at me and turned back to Aunt Connie. "Like I said, you don't need to worry, Little Sis. We'll catch whoever did this, but we're going to need your help. Now, you just take it nice and slow-like, think about it a bit, and tell us whatever you remember."

"I've been thinking about it, Rudd. It's all I can think about." Aunt Connie squeezed her eyes shut. "I just can't remember much of anything after Aaron called me on the phone last night."

"He called? I didn't know that. What did he say?" Uncle Rudd prodded.

"He just said he needed to talk to me." Aunt Connie opened her eyes and shrugged. "Said he wanted to explain things, and he could make it all up to me, if I gave him a chance. I wasn't too nice at first. I made it clear that he was forty years too late, the flowers were already wilted, and I sold my wedding dress years ago. But he kept on begging real pretty-like until I finally gave in. I was working late on some flower arrangements, so I told him to come to the back door of the shop. After we hung up I thought that I ought to run upstairs to my apartment and fix up a little. I know that's vanity, plain and simple, but I wanted to look nice for this big explanation he was gonna give me." She paused for a moment, then continued with trembling voice. "I remember comin' back down the stairs, but after that, I don't remember much of anything, except that Aaron was dead."

It was more than Aunt Connie could bear. She put her hands to her face and began to cry. Aunt Nissa produced a box of tissues, and as Aunt Connie wept, Aunt Nissa steadily pulled one tissue after another out of the box and handed them to her. I put my arm around her, and we let her cry it out.

Finally Aunt Connie blew her nose, and slowly shaking her head, spoke directly to Uncle Rudd. "The next thing

I remember is being in the car with Nissa. I must've been plumb out of my head or something."

I gave Aunt Connie a reassuring squeeze and told her that sometimes shock and grief can make us forget parts of things that happen to us. It's the mind's way of protecting us from being overwhelmed.

She looked up at me. "You think that's it, Dixie, you really think that's what's wrong?"

"Yes, I do, and you don't have to try and remember right now." I shot my uncle a warning look, just in case he had other ideas. "With time, and when you're able to deal with it, then it will all come back to you. Don't try to force it."

Blowing her nose once more, she sighed. "I'm sorry, Rudd. Let's hope Dixie is right and I will remember. But right now there's nothing else I can tell you."

Defeated, Uncle Rudd handed her another tissue. "That's all right, Baby Sister, you did just fine. At least we know more than we did last night. For one thing you remembered the phone call from him." Suddenly Uncle Rudd slammed his hand down on the table. "But it sure would have been nice if before he died that piece of pestilence would've explained that little disappearing act he did just before the wedding."

This outburst only made Aunt Connie cry all the harder. With one hand Aunt Nissa handed Aunt Connie yet another tissue, and with the other she smacked Uncle Rudd on the back of the head, just to let him know what an insensitive brute he was.

Aunt Connie sputtered in between sobs. "Don't talk about him like that, Rudd. I'd like to know why he left, too. But isn't it more important right now that we find out who killed him and why?"

"I'm sorry, Little Sis, I didn't mean to upset you." Uncle Rudd glanced over at Aunt Nissa as if to make sure she kept her hands to herself. "I guess it was pretty stupid of me to say it like that. It's just that I think it might be possible that his running away before the wedding is somehow, someway connected to him being murdered."

"How do you figure that, dear?" Aunt Nissa asked.

"I admit I never really liked old Aaron, but he did show a healthy spark of good sense when he started courtin' Connie. And I have to admit that he always seemed downright crazy in love with her. So I was just as surprised as anybody when he didn't show up for the wedding. I never figured him for the running kind. Now, I'm thinking something pretty important scared him and made him run. If that's the case, I don't know what made him think it was safe for him to come back into town after all these years. Whatever his reason, he figured wrong, and it got him killed."

"You might have a good point, Rudd. I sure don't know the answers to either one of those questions, but there's one thing I need to know." Aunt Connie leaned forward as far as she could. "I gotta know why you think I didn't kill Aaron. How do you know that I didn't just go plumb loony and stab him myself? Maybe I am the guilty one that murdered him."

Uncle Rudd leaned forward and met her almost nose-to-nose. "First off, Connie Tanner, you ain't got a murderin' bone in your scrawny little body, no matter how crazy you get. You used to cry when our fishin' worms died. And second," Uncle Rudd picked up a piece of paper with his handwriting on it and held it up in front of Aunt Connie's face, "you said so last night. I got it all right here. I wrote down everything you said. Most of it I can't make heads or tails out of, but one thing you kept saying over and over was, and I quote, 'The boogeyman came out of the night and killed my Aaron, the boogeyman covered my Aaron in blood.' Don't you see, Little Sis, you ain't talking 'bout yourself. Someone else did the killin'."

Aunt Connie let out a sigh of relief and sat back in her chair. "In my heart I didn't think I could do such a horrible thing. But since I can't remember, it's a comfort to hear you say I didn't."

"Now that we're clear on that point," Uncle Rudd nodded, pushing the piece of paper he was holding toward me, "we got to find out who did do it. That's all the stuff Connie said last night. Take a look at it, Dixie-gal, and see if you can make anything of it."

All three of them were silent as I took the paper and looked at it. Except for the part about Aaron being covered in blood, it really was just a jumble of nonsensical words. I kept looking at the paper because it gave me time to think.

If this letter-size piece of paper was all we had to go on to find a killer, we were in a lot of trouble. I had no idea what the sentence for obstructing justice might be, but I'm quite certain that hiding a dead body would constitute more than parole and a hefty fine. So, for the time being, I still clung to the notion that the sheriff should handle this. Besides, there was one other little problem concerning the body of Aaron Scott that I had yet to hear anybody address.

Deciding to meet the problem head-on and give reason another shot, I looked at Uncle Rudd. "These are words of grief and trauma. I don't know that we can decipher them as quickly as you might have hoped. Considering that time is a factor here, maybe we should have some sort of backup plan. I don't know where you hid Aaron Scott's body, but there are limits to. . .well. . .you know, limits to how long before his body does what all dead bodies do. And let's face it, we may not have found the murderer by then."

Although discussing dead bodies is not even close to my idea of good conversation, Aunt Nissa took the bait. "What did you have in mind as a backup plan, dear?"

Before I could take advantage of the opening she gave me, Uncle Rudd spoke up. "I got a pretty good idea what our Dixie-gal here has in mind for a backup plan." He looked me in the eye and pointed his finger. "We will not let Sheriff Otis in on this until we get the goods on whoever killed Aaron Scott. And there is no need for you to go worryin' over that body either. Let's just say it's hidden someplace where he'll still look every bit as dead as the night he got himself murdered."

I sat there trying very hard not to throw my hands up in the air in defeat. Although wildly curious as to where Uncle Rudd hid Aaron Scott's body, I concentrated on what and how to say the right thing that would make my uncle listen to reason. But whatever embryonic thoughts I had forming in my head at the time were loudly interrupted by a knock at the front door.

Aunt Nissa had the foresight to lean back in her chair and pull a corner of her red gingham curtains up so she could see who was at the front door. "Uh-oh, it's Sheriff Otis, and he's in uniform."

As soon as Aunt Connie heard who was at the front door, she threw her arms on the kitchen table with her wrists together as if she had on handcuffs and moaned, "He's come to take me away, Rudd. He's found my poor Aaron. There's nothin' you can do for me now. This here was my last meal, my last morsel of home-cooked food."

No one ran to the door to let Otis in right away. Instead, Aunt Nissa jumped out of her chair and put a protective arm around Aunt Connie. Uncle Rudd was busy stuffing his file folder and legal pad into Aunt Nissa's silverware drawer. And me? I was enjoying the feeling of relief that Sheriff Otis Beecher had come to the rescue.

"Oh, Rudd," Aunt Nissa whispered, "you said no one would ever find Aaron's body. How could Sheriff Otis stumble onto it so soon?"

"I don't know what he's here for, but I seriously doubt he

found that body," Uncle Rudd answered. "Let's not panic yet. Nissa, you take Connie and go on upstairs. And stay real quiet, ya hear?"

Both aunts, arm in arm, obediently headed upstairs.

Uncle Rudd yelled, "Just a minute" toward the front door then turned to me and said, "Dixie-gal, if you say anything to Otis about this murder, I'll make sure that none of us ever speak to you again. Not only that, I'll call your folks and tell them what happened. They won't be one bit pleased that you brought Otis in on this. Remember, Tanners stick together."

That threat might not work in some families, but it does in the Tanner clan. As much as my family exasperated me, I didn't want to be ostracized. I wanted it to be my idea to move to a deserted island. I'd keep my mouth shut.

Uncle Rudd and Otis came into the kitchen laughing about something or other. I had personally never seen Otis at work in an official capacity, but I figured if he really knew what my uncle was up to, he wouldn't find it at all amusing.

Still smiling, Uncle Rudd gave Otis a little slap on the back. "Have a seat. I'll get you a cup of coffee. Dixie, you want some more coffee?"

I nodded, keeping my mouth shut as ordered.

Otis put his hat on the table and took the chair opposite me. "Hey, Dixie, nice to see you back in town. Still like living in the big city?"

"Oh yes," I said. Short answers are almost as good as keeping one's mouth shut.

"When did you get into town?"

"This morning." I wasn't too bad at this short answer stuff.

Otis moved around in his chair until he was sitting sideways and could stretch out. One of the most notable things about our sheriff is that he is six foot, five inches tall, and most of that is legs.

"Thanks." Otis nodded as he took the cup from Uncle Rudd. He took a sip then reached into his shirt pocket and pulled out a small notepad and a pen. "Actually, I'm here on sort of an official visit. I need to ask Connie a few questions, and she wasn't at her apartment, so I was wondering if she was out here?"

At that moment we all heard a disturbing thudding noise coming from upstairs. It abruptly stopped, but out of instinct, all three of us looked up.

Uncle Rudd didn't acknowledge the interruption. "Well now, Otis, you came to the right place. Connie's here with us. Has been since last night. But she's not feeling a bit good. No sir, not a bit good. We thought she could use a little catering to and rest. How official is this visit?"

Otis shrugged. "I don't guess it's official enough to drag her out of her sickbed. Maybe you can help me out, Rudd. Considering how fast news travels around here, I'm assuming you know that Aaron Scott showed up in town yesterday?"

"Yeah, we heard." Uncle Rudd's thick eyebrows knitted together. "But it's not likely we'd invite that little troll over for a nice chat over Sunday dinner."

"Wouldn't expect you to." Otis chuckled. "My questions concern a phone call I got last night."

Otis suddenly stopped talking and sat there slouching in his chair like the urge to contemplate the mysteries of the universe had just overtaken him. I wondered if he used that "suddenly silent" technique on any of the criminals he arrested. I know I felt compelled to fill in the silence with everything I knew. It was only the fear of being thrown out of the family that kept me quiet.

Uncle Rudd got up and poured himself another cup of coffee and sat back down. "Now, Otis, you gonna tell us about this phone call, or is this one of those things you ain't allowed to talk about?"

"Guess it won't hurt none to say." Otis shrugged. "Around nine o'clock I received one of those anonymous phone calls, you know, where the person disguises their voice. The caller said that I should hurry down to the Red Carnations Flower Shop because there would likely be some fireworks between Connie and Aaron. Then the caller hung up. I don't put a lot of stock in those kind of calls, but I thought maybe Connie might still be of a mind to throw a flowerpot or two at old Aaron, so I headed out to the flower shop."

Otis stopped talking again. They must teach that stuff in some kind of sheriff's seminar. The suspense was almost too much for me. I could feel the tic near my left eye start to thump. I had no idea what time Uncle Rudd found Aunt

Connie and Aaron, but Otis must have just missed them. Otherwise all of them would be in jail by now, and I would be scraping up bail money. It also hit me that whoever murdered Aaron had called Otis to try and frame Aunt Connie. I had a sick feeling in the pit of my stomach. For the first time since Uncle Rudd called, I began to entertain the idea that he was right about going after the killer ourselves. Of course, I have entertained bad ideas before.

Uncle Rudd shook his head slowly. "I reckon it was just some joker trying to cause a little trouble. But I can honestly say that Connie didn't throw any flowerpots at Aaron. No, sir, somewhere between nine and nine thirty last night we were heading home with her. We must've just missed you."

"Naw," Otis drawled, "we missed each other by quite a bit, since I never made it to Connie's place. I was on my way, when I came up on an accident. Old Dennis Reager had a row with his wife last night and was heading out to stay at his brother's trailer until Rosa May cooled down. He forgot we put a stop sign up on Lincoln Street not too long ago. Truman Spencer was behind Ed Baringer at the stop sign, when Dennis smacked right into Truman's new SUV, forcing Truman to smack into Baringer's truck. No one was really hurt, unless you count the swollen lip old Truman got from Dennis throwing a punch at him."

"Is that a fact?" Uncle Rudd grinned.

"Yeah, it was somethin' all right." Otis grinned back. "By the time I got there, Truman was fit to be tied. He started pokin' his finger on Dennis's chest and threatening to sue him. Told Dennis he'd own that new tractor of his. 'Course, you know Dennis, he's more partial to farm machinery than he is to Rosa May, so he just up and let Spencer have it right in the kisser."

Uncle Rudd chuckled. "You know as well as I do Truman has always had a big mouth."

"Suppose so. Anyway, I didn't get through settling them down and filling out all the paperwork till near eleven that night. I figured if there was any trouble between Connie and Aaron, I would've heard about it by then, so I just went on home." Otis stood up and stretched. "Speaking of home, I'd better head on out of here. Martha's got some kinfolk coming over for supper tonight, and I told her I'd stop by the grocery store and pick up some celery and hamburger meat." He walked over and put his coffee cup in the sink. "Thanks for the coffee, Rudd. You're probably right about that phone call. Someone was just hoping for a little fireworks to gossip about. By the way, what did happen when Connie and Aaron got together last night?"

I almost got whiplash turning my head so I could get a good look at Uncle Rudd's face.

He never flexed a muscle when he said, "As far as I know, they did their talking on the phone."

Accepting Uncle Rudd's answer, Otis waved a hand goodbye. "Don't bother gettin' up Rudd, I reckon I can see myself out the door. See y'all later. Stop in and see Martha if you get a chance, Dixie."

We heard the door shut, and both of us huddled up by the window so we could watch Otis pull out the driveway.

"We'd better get on upstairs, Dixie-gal," Uncle Rudd said. "Since we heard that one noise coming from upstairs, they've been awful quiet up there. Too quiet, if you ask me."

CHAPTER FOUR

As soon as we saw Otis's taillights, Uncle Rudd and I bolted up the stairs.

We found them in the blue room. Aunt Nissa was placidly rocking back and forth in an old sewing rocker, quilting on what looked like a pillow top. Aunt Connie, on the other hand, was not nearly as placid. She was busy wriggling around on the bed, all neatly bound and gagged with colorful scraps of quilting material. Her dark green flower-print dress was hiked up past her bony knees, exposing two scrawny-looking legs encased in rolled-up stockings.

I was speechless.

Uncle Rudd was not. "Good grief, Nissa, did you have to truss her up like a chicken?"

Aunt Nissa shrugged. Then jutting her chin out, she answered, "Don't get huffy with me, Rudd Tanner. Connie had another one of her spells. I didn't know what else to do. You said to keep her quiet, so I did the best I could with what I had."

Uncle Rudd patted Nissa on the shoulder. "Now, don't

get upset, honey. I know you did what you had to do."

Since neither of them seemed the least bit inclined to untie my trussed-up aunt, I decided to do the job myself.

I started toward her, but Uncle Rudd grabbed my arm before I could begin untying her. "I wouldn't do that just yet," he warned.

"The sheriff is gone. You can't possibly leave her like this." I looked at my poor aunt wrapped up in everything from stripes to gingham to checks. "If you won't untie her, I will!"

Uncle Rudd gripped my arm tighter. "Maybe you should sit down for a minute, and let's talk about it."

I jerked my arm away from him and huffed. "Aunt Connie needs to be untied right this minute. Then we can talk."

It is my belief that I huff very well. After all, I have seen Tanner aunts, uncles, cousins, and parents do it for years.

Uncle Rudd started talking as fast as he could. "Wait! Look at her eyes, Dixie-gal. They look like they did last night when Nissa and I found her. Nissa's right, I think she's having one of them spells like she did last night. Maybe we ought not to be so quick to untie her."

I peered around Uncle Rudd and looked at Aunt Connie's eyes. I had to admit they were frantic and darting, but that didn't mean she was having a "spell." I couldn't help but think that if I were bound and gagged with all that material, my eyes would be frantic and darting, too. "Uncle Rudd, she's scared, that's all."

"You'd better tell her how Connie has been acting the past few months, Rudd," Aunt Nissa said quietly, but firmly.

A look of indecision crossed over Uncle Rudd's face, so I encouraged him. "Aunt Connie's been acting differently lately? How?"

"Well now, we don't rightly know what's going on with her, but she's been confused and forgetting a lot of things lately. She's been drivin' Peggy, the little gal that works for her, plumb nuts. At first we figured it was just age, but it seems like lately it's a little more often than normal."

"Have you taken her to see Doc Mayfair?" I asked.

"It was sure enough almost a dog fight, but Nissa and I insisted she see Doc last week," Uncle Rudd replied. "He wanted her to go over to the hospital at Brogan's Ferry so they could run some tests. Connie wouldn't hear of it. She and Doc got into one of their shoutin' matches. Finally Doc said he guessed he'd just have to wait until she lost all her marbles and couldn't tell who she was before he could figure out what's wrong."

"But she could be having mild strokes, or getting senile, or a hundred other things," I wailed. "She has to go have those tests."

At that moment Aunt Connie began wiggling with all her might and managed to wiggle right off the bed, landing on the floor with a *thud*.

In one swift fluid movement, Uncle Rudd reached down and picked her up like she weighed no more than a ten-pound sack of potatoes and plopped her right back on the bed. Then he looked at me like nothing had happened. "We've tried our best to get her to go for those tests, but she's a might stubborn."

I was so stunned at Uncle Rudd's actions, I failed to notice that Aunt Nissa was trying to talk to me until I felt her gently tugging at my arm to get my attention. When I looked at her she smiled shyly and said, "Dixie dear, why don't you have a little talk with Connie about having those tests run? Rudd and I have tried everything we know to do. We even asked Pastor Jeff to talk with her, and all I can say about that incident is that he truly is a forgiving man. She might listen to what you have to say, though. After all, you're a psychologist, dear. It certainly couldn't hurt to try."

"That's a great idea," Uncle Rudd added. "And while you're at it, see if she remembers anything else about the murder yet. Nissa and I will be out on the front porch."

They scooted out of the room and shut the door before I could yell, "Help, I'm being held hostage by my relatives!"

I looked at Aunt Connie and decided that I would untie her hands first, so that she could help me get the rest of the quilting strips off her. That was a mistake. As soon as her hands were free, I felt a sharp sting on my cheek and my head jolted back. In one swift motion she had slapped my face. Out of self-defense I grabbed both her wrists and kept a firm hold on them. As calmly as possible I said to her, "Aunt Connie. I'm not going to hurt you. Now, if you'll stay calm,

I'll untie you. You have to promise me that you'll keep your hands and any other parts of your body to yourself. If you agree, blink twice."

Her body relaxed, and she blinked twice. I carefully let go of her wrists and held my breath. She folded her arms across her chest and stayed very still. I breathed a little easier. She was going to cooperate.

Aunt Nissa had done an excellent job. I'd have to ask her how she got Aunt Connie to stay still long enough to tie her up. As near as I could figure, the quilt pieces must have already been on the bed. Then, remembering that in her younger days Aunt Nissa could rope and tie a calf better than most men, I formed a mental picture in my mind of Aunt Nissa throwing Aunt Connie on the bed and landing on her like she would a calf at a rodeo. Briefly, I tried to calculate how long it actually took Aunt Nissa to tie her up. Did it take one minute? Two? Couldn't have taken very long, according to the thumps we had heard downstairs.

Getting back to the business at hand, I said softly, "I'm going to untie your ankles now."

Slowly I moved to the end of the bed to untie the bright yellow quilt piece that was wound around her ankles. I jumped back a little, but she didn't try to kick me. So far so good, I thought.

The gag around her mouth was next. I braced myself and untied the gag and took out all the stuffing Aunt Nissa had managed to put in her mouth.

She laid there, eyes looking straight ahead. She was so still it worried me.

Gently shaking her shoulder, I said, "Aunt Connie, are you all right? Can you hear me?"

She slowly turned her head toward me and whispered, "If you don't watch out, the boogeyman is gonna cover you in red."

Uh-oh, I was about to experience one of Aunt Connie's so called "spells" firsthand.

I wondered if I should go to the window and call Uncle Rudd and Aunt Nissa back upstairs. I started to get up, but Aunt Connie grabbed my arms so tight her fingernails dug into my flesh.

"Be careful, Dixie," she moaned, "or the boogeyman will get you, just like he got my Aaron. All covered in red carnations. There were so many he couldn't breathe." She suddenly let go of my arm and brushed her hands up and down her chest, moaning in a low, eerie voice, "No breath, no breath, all gone, and not even a blue note. No blue note, just gone."

Was this waking nightmare she was experiencing her response to trauma? It was certainly probable. Was there something else in addition to the trauma going on? Possibly. I just didn't have an answer.

Wanting to do whatever I could to help her, I shuffled around on the bed until I could put my arms around her. Gently rocking her back and forth, I whispered in her ear,

"Don't worry, I'll take you to see Doc Mayfair first thing tomorrow morning. He can set up those tests, and I will take you over to the hospital myself. I promise I will stay with you every minute; you don't have to be afraid."

Wallowing in frustration and helplessness, I held her tighter and buried my head on her shoulder.

Never one to abide anyone's wallowing, Aunt Connie pushed my head aside and gruffly said, "Stop it, you dummy, you're choking me." Apparently she was herself again. The sudden flip-flop from crazy to cranky was startling. Waving a spindly finger in my direction, she added, "Don't think for one minute you're going to weasel me into going to that hospital. I don't need to spend my hard-earned money letting some doctor tell me I'm crazy. Rudd and Nissa tell me that all the time for free."

"But maybe there is more to this than just trauma," I sputtered. "Maybe there's some sort of treatment or medication that would help you."

"Phooey, ain't nothin' but old age. After all, I am in my late fifties, though of course I don't look it."

Aunt Connie was the youngest of the Tanner offspring from my grandparents, and by my calculations she was sixty-two, but I didn't argue with her about that. Instead I focused on the most important issue. "You still need to see Doc Mayfair and let him give you a good physical. Trauma may not be the only thing going on with your mind and body."

I might as well have been talking to the old oak tree out

by the driveway, because all she said was, "Where's Nissa?"

I gave up for the time being and followed her lead. "She's out on the front porch with Uncle Rudd."

Aunt Connie looked around and sighed. "I guess I must've had one of them spells and run her off."

"You didn't run her off. But you were having a pretty rough time. They just thought they would give us time together and maybe I could help you. Do you remember anything at all about this episode?"

"Episode?" She rolled the word around on her tongue several times like she was infatuated with it. "'Episode.' I like that word, 'episode.' Doesn't make me sound so crazy when you say 'episode' does it? And no, I don't remember anything about my episode. I never do. What'd I say?"

I was afraid to give her the details. Afraid it might send her back to that dark corner of her mind at worst, and at best, worry her even more than she was already. I shrugged my shoulders and said, "Nothing much, you just talked about red carnations and a blue note."

"Blue note." The words were spoken so softly I almost didn't hear what she said.

"Do you know what 'blue note' means?"

"Of course not! I was having an episode, remember?" She vigorously shook her head and changed the subject. "But I do remember Otis was here. What did he want? Did he find the body?"

Aunt Connie's eyes widened a little when I finished

telling her about Otis's visit. She bit down on one of her fingernails and seemed to be thinking about the close call they had last night.

"So, if I'm understanding this right," she said, "whoever killed my Aaron tried to get Otis there in time to pin it on me."

"Looks that way." I nodded

"Well, I'll be hornswoggled. Rudd's right about this, ain't he? We'll have to find out who killed Aaron ourselves. Well now, if I'm gonna help with this family investigation, I need my beauty sleep. You go on out and tell Rudd and Nissa that after I take a nap I'm going straight on back to my place." Having said her piece, Aunt Connie pulled the blue and white dove-in-a-window quilt at the end of the bed all the way up to her chin. "Now, go on, git," she commanded and waved her hand toward the door then rolled over and closed her eyes.

Oh joy, now she not only approved of Uncle Rudd taking the law into his own hands, she planned to help! I stayed beside her for a few more minutes. When she started snoring I got up and tiptoed out the door.

Aunt Nissa and Uncle Rudd were sitting side by side, holding hands, on the front porch swing. Aunt Nissa motioned for me to sit down on the wooden rocker nearby. "I laid an afghan there for you, dear. It's a little chilly out here. How's Connie?"

I slid into the rocker, pulled the afghan around my

shoulders like a shawl, and told them everything that happened after they ducked and ran, including the part about the red carnations and the blue note.

When I finished talking, Uncle Rudd heaved a heavy sigh. "I think you're right about blood looking like red carnations to Connie, but I don't have any more notion than you do about what that blue note is about."

"I might," Aunt Nissa said quietly. "I mean, I know what it reminds me of, anyway. Rudd, you remember the day Connie was supposed to get married."

"I do." Uncle Rudd huffed. "One of the blackest days in Tanner history. Why that spineless excuse for. . ."

"Yes, I know, dear," Aunt Nissa gently interrupted. "But what I was getting at was that Aaron sent a bouquet of handpicked red carnations and a letter to Connie. I was with her when she opened the letter. The note was written on light blue paper. I was thinking that maybe the blue note Connie referred to upstairs must have something to do with the Dear Jane note that he sent to her on her wedding day."

"Why, you wonderful woman!" Uncle Rudd reached over and hugged her. "We might just have our first clue. What'd the note say?"

"I'm sorry, dear. I don't know what the note said. Connie never let anyone read it that I know of."

I watched Uncle Rudd's face fall and his shoulders slump in discouragement. He was so sure that we would have three or four good clues before bedtime and be hot on the trail of the killer by dawn. I felt so sorry for him that I opened my mouth without first asking permission from my brain. "Look, you both know that Aunt Connie doesn't like to throw things away. She even leaves bologna in the refrigerator long enough for the stuff to learn rudimentary sign language. Surely she would save the last letter from the love of her life, even if that letter were painful to read. She probably stuck it somewhere in her apartment."

Uncle Rudd's face lit up. "You're absolutely right! And I have just the job for you. You said that Connie wants to go back to her place tonight, right?"

"That's what she said," I dutifully answered.

"Good, then you can go back to her apartment with her. After she goes to sleep, you poke around some, see if you can find that note."

"Uh, wouldn't it be a lot easier if we just asked her for the note?" It seemed to me that my uncle was going about this the hard way.

"Of course it would!" he bellowed. "But we can't do that. It might send her into one of those spells again. We got to protect her as much as possible."

We spent the next twenty or so minutes arguing about whether or not asking Aunt Connie for the note would send her into another "spell." I didn't think it would; Uncle Rudd did. In the end, we compromised. I agreed to spend the night with Aunt Connie and skulk around for the note.

Uncle Rudd agreed to let me drive his beloved, fully restored, 1967 white Mustang with baby blue interior, until he could get my Jeep fixed.

I had only driven the '67 Mustang one other time. That was five years ago. Uncle Rudd let me drive it up and down their half-mile driveway while he sat in the passenger seat, dictating precise instructions on how to drive an automatic and yelling that fifteen miles an hour was way too fast.

Of course there was one other person that Uncle Rudd had to convince. And that made for lively conversation between him and Aunt Connie at the supper table that night. Nevertheless, Uncle Rudd won, and I would be spending the night with Aunt Connie.

As we were standing on the front porch saying good night, Aunt Nissa handed me a pie and slipped a sack of quilting material under my arm. She whispered, "Pie's for eatin'. The other. . .just in case. . .another spell. . ."

Aunt Connie whipped the sack out from under my arm and handed it back to Aunt Nissa, saying, "I don't need to be tied up. And quit calling 'em spells. 'Spells' sounds stupid. Dixie calls them episodes. I told you at supper I want everybody to call them episodes. Episodes!"

Before she could work herself into another "episode," I grabbed Aunt Connie's arm and we headed out to the garage where Uncle Rudd had the Mustang warmed up for us.

Aunt Connie settled herself in the passenger seat, and I went around to the driver's side where Uncle Rudd was standing. Before I could open the door and dash inside, he stopped me and in a low voice said, "Whatever you do, don't let Connie work on any flower arrangements tonight."

That was certainly not what I had expected him to say. I had braced myself for a lecture on all things Mustang. Confused, I asked, "Why not?"

It was eight o'clock in the evening. We would be at Aunt Connie's in less than twenty minutes. A little work might be good for her, take her mind off things. Then it hit me that working in the flower shop might not be the best way to work off tension after all. I was glad that Uncle Rudd was sensitive to Aunt Connie's plight and said to him, "Oh, I get it! You don't want her down there in the workshop where the murder took place right now because it might be too hard on her emotionally."

"Uh, yeah, that's right, Dixie-gal. It'd be too hard on her, ya see." Then he practically shoved me into the driver's seat and added, "You remember what I said now. Well, you'd better get going." Then he shut the door and waved good-bye.

Overjoyed at not getting one of Uncle Rudd's Mustang lectures, I waved gaily back and pulled out of the garage. It never occurred to me to question his motives.

We were pretty quiet on the way into town. Which suited me, because I was busy trying to figure out just how I had managed to get sucked into becoming an accessory to murder in such a short period of time. I didn't even know where they hid the body.

As I pulled into the alley behind Aunt Connie's flower shop, I noticed that the lights were on in the smaller apartment next to hers. Years ago, after she had opened up her flower shop downstairs, she had bought the building and had the upstairs turned into two apartments, with a staircase in the back leading up to a long porch and the apartments. She kept the smaller of the two apartments rented whenever she could.

As we were getting out of the car, I said, "Last time I was in town, you were having trouble finding a renter. I see you found one. Anyone I know?"

"Nope, nobody you'd know," Aunt Connie said. "The man's new in town. Rented that apartment two months ago. He's an artist. Works with wood. Carves with knives mostly, but sometimes he uses a chainsaw. Pretty good at it. Sends his stuff off to fancy art galleries in places like California and Florida. Gets some hefty prices for those carvings of his."

"Really! Maybe I've seen his work. What's his name?"

"Name's Freedom Crane. Sort of a strange name. He said his parents named him that because they bought a coffee shop named Freedom Grove in some town in California two days before he was born." Aunt Connie stopped at the top of the staircase. Turning around to face me, she flashed me a sly grin. "He's only a little older than you, and he's single. Want me to introduce you?"

Oh, great. Just what I needed. A moody artistic type who knows how to handle knives and chainsaws. "Not on your life," I replied and shuffled her into her apartment as fast as I could. The last thing I needed was Aunt Connie in cahoots with Aunt Nissa to find me Mr. Right.

I settled into what Aunt Connie loosely refers to as her guest room. The room is no bigger than an extra-large closet, with one round window facing the alley. The only furniture in the room is a daybed and an antique wardrobe.

Dutifully remembering that I was there to ferret out the blue note, I poked through the drawers in the wardrobe. As I shoved the last drawer back into place, I decided that Uncle Rudd was wrong. The best thing to do would be to ask Aunt Connie about the note the first opportunity I got.

I showered, put on my favorite pink flannel pajamas, and walked into the living room just as Aunt Connie hung up the phone.

Without my having to ask, Aunt Connie explained, "I overheard Rudd telling you not to let me go down to the workshop. I thought I'd make things easy on all of us, and I called Peggy. She's coming in tonight to finish the flower arrangements for Tance Larribee's Bed and Breakfast. When she's finished, she'll take them on home with her tonight and deliver them in the morning."

I grinned sheepishly at her and said, "I guess Uncle Rudd never could whisper very well."

"There's been a time or two, when the wind's just right, that I'm pretty sure that voice of his carried into the next county." She giggled.

I couldn't help it, I giggled right along with her.

On a roll, Aunt Connie sputtered between giggles. "Your dad always said that Rudd could stand on top of any hill and become his own radio station. We even made up call letters for him, W-L-O-U-D."

That did it. We laughed until we had to hold on to each other. It really wasn't that funny. But it was laugh or cry time. We chose to laugh.

With both of us in a much better humor, Aunt Connie asked if I would play a couple of hands of gin rummy with her before we went to bed. I not only said I would play, I offered to cut us each a piece of the apple pie that Aunt Nissa sent home with us while Aunt Connie got the cards out. Besides, I thought it might give me an opportunity to ask about the note.

We never got to finish that first game of gin rummy, or our pie. We were interrupted by a high piercing scream that ended abruptly. A scream that came from downstairs.

CHAPTER FIVE

Aunt Connie jumped up from the table so fast cards scattered everywhere. "Peggy! That scream must've come from Peggy downstairs."

I made it to the door first. On my way out, I told Aunt Connie to stay put in case she needed to call Sheriff Otis or an ambulance.

I heard her say, "Fat chance," just as I ran into someone on the porch. I had enough presence of mind to note that it must be the new renter. There wasn't time for polite introductions. We shoved and pushed our way downstairs with Aunt Connie hot on our heels.

The renter got to the door of the flower shop first and pulled frantically on the doorknob. Like the hysterical person that I was at the time, I accentuated the obvious by wringing my hands and yelling, "It's locked! The door's locked. We forgot the keys."

"Maybe you forgot, but I didn't." Aunt Connie pulled the keys out of the side pocket of her dress. "Now get out of my way, you two."

We parted like the Red Sea and let her through. She deftly put in the key and opened the door. All three of us tried to go through at once. We grunted and shoved until we were inside the workroom of the flower shop.

Peggy's tall frame was sprawled on the floor in front of the opened door to the flower cooler. Aunt Connie got on her knees and looked Peggy over carefully, then informed us, "I think she just fainted. She might be sick, but in the five years she's worked for me, I've never known her to faint. Guess there's a first time for everything."

"Uh, I'm pretty sure I know what made her faint," the renter muttered. "And I think we'd better work fast if we don't want the sheriff breathing down our necks."

Moving quickly to the front of the shop, the renter called back, "I've got an idea, so don't try bringing her around just yet. We've only got a few minutes as it is."

"Do you know what that man is talking about?" I asked Aunt Connie. "What did you tell me his name is?"

"Name's Freedom," she answered. "I don't know exactly what he's up to, but since I can feel the air to the flower cooler is a lot colder than it should be, I got my suspicions."

Aunt Connie stepped over the passed-out Peggy and peered into the cooler. Her hand flew to her mouth. "Oh, my. They really did put him in the flower cooler."

Stupidly, I asked, "Who put who where?"

Then it dawned on me. I put two and two together and came up with one dead body, one demented relative, and one very helpful renter. The scenario went something like this: poor Peggy screamed and fainted because late last night they, meaning my uncle, the Demented One, and his new pal, Freedom, the Helpful Renter, had put Aaron Scott, the Dead Body, in the flower cooler.

Of all the harebrained things that generations of Tanners have done—and believe me we can trace our peculiar brand of insanity back for fourteen generations—this had to be the most outrageous, Tenacious Tanner not withstanding.

Freedom came back to the workroom carrying the life-size scarecrow that had been a large part of Aunt Connie's harvesttime window display.

Handing me the scarecrow, he said, "Hold this, while I get Scott's body out of the cooler."

"Just what am I supposed to do with this thing?" I demanded.

Freedom leaned close to Aunt Connie and me and in a low voice said, "Look, there's not a lot of time. You two wrap that scarecrow in some of that pink cellophane Connie keeps over there in the corner. I'm going to take Scott out of the cooler and put him in the bed of my truck. I think I know a place where we can hide him until we're sure it's safe to put him back in the cooler. Once you get that scarecrow wrapped, put it in the cooler where Scott was. Hopefully we can get Scott and the scarecrow switched by the time Peggy comes to." Then he dashed into the cooler.

"Pink cellophane! Why pink cellophane?" I asked. Surely

they didn't wrap him up in pink cellophane.

Oh yes, they did! Freedom came out with the body of Aaron Scott wrapped in pink cellophane on his shoulder.

Now I knew why Uncle Rudd didn't want me to let Aunt Connie in the workshop tonight. He didn't want her to find the body. He couldn't have foreseen that Aunt Connie would call Peggy in to finish up the flower arrangements. But she did, and now we had to deal with Peggy finding the body.

"Don't just stand there with your mouth open, Dixie June. We got to get that scarecrow wrapped up now!" Aunt Connie hissed.

She already had a wad of cellophane in her hand, trying to wrap it around the scarecrow. I closed my mouth and grabbed the end to help her.

By the time we had the scarecrow wrapped up, Freedom had come back in, and we helped him put it in the same spot they had put Aaron's body the night before.

As we hurried out of the cooler, Peggy, still a little groggy, was propped up on one arm. When she saw us, her eyes widened and she pointed to the cooler, stammering, "St–Stay out of there. B–Body, dead body. I saw it. Call Otis, q–quick!"

"Now, take it easy, dear. There's nothing like that in the cooler," Aunt Connie said quietly, but firmly. "Only thing in there is that old six-foot scarecrow I usually have in the front window. Go on and look for yourself."

Peggy got to her feet and looked at each one of us like we

had taken leave of our senses. Which, of course we had.

With a dazed expression still on her face, Peggy pulled herself up straight and said defensively, "I know what I saw. If you don't believe me, you just march right in there and take another look for yourself. I tell you, there's a dead body in that cooler, and it's all wrapped in pink cellophane!"

Apparently, the twenty-something Peggy Bannan was not aware of the Tanner propensity for peculiar behavior. Peggy and her husband moved here seven years ago. You would have thought that in a small town like Kenna Springs someone would've had the decency to warn her.

With a shrug of his shoulders, Freedom said, "Okay, I'll look," and walked into the cooler. When he came out with the scarecrow in his arms, Peggy scuttled around the other end of the worktable in the center of the room.

"That's it! That's what I saw." Peggy squeaked and pointed.

Grinning, Freedom loosened the wrapping around the head and said, "See, Peggy, it's just a scarecrow."

"A scarecrow! But. . ." Out of instinct Peggy turned her head toward the unlit showroom window then back to us. "But the scarecrow was in the window. How did it get in the cooler?"

"I must've put it in there," Aunt Connie admitted.

"Why?" she asked.

Aunt Connie shrugged her shoulders. "Why do I do anything lately?"

"Oh," was all Peggy said, but I knew by the look on her

face that she now assumed Aunt Connie was more confused than ever.

"Well, now that that's settled," Aunt Connie said, "I'll help Peggy finish up, while you go on upstairs and change clothes, Dixie."

"Change clothes? Why?"

"Mercy child, have you already forgotten? Mr. Crane here offered to take you to get some ice cream for that apple pie Nissa sent home with us. And you certainly can't go in your flannel pajamas, now can you?"

She beamed at me with such innocence I wanted to spit. Nonetheless, I was shooed out of the workroom and found my little self standing outside in the alley with Mr. Freedom Crane, along with the body of Aaron Scott wrapped in pink cellophane, stretched out in the bed of a truck.

Grinning at me, Freedom said, "I guess since we'll be spending some time together, you ought to know that even though we haven't been introduced, I'm a friend of the family. Rudd called me awhile ago to fill me in on things and asked if I would keep an eye on you and Connie. In fact, I was on my way over to Connie's place to meet you when I heard the scream." He stuck his hand out. "My name's Freedom Crane and I. . ."

"I already know your name," I interrupted, ignoring his outstretched hand. "I also know that you must be quite daft to get involved in this mess. And the only reason we will be spending time together is because Aunt Connie obviously thinks you need some help carting Mr. Scott around. So, if you'll excuse me, I'll go and change and we can get this over with."

Although I didn't think I was a bit funny, I was halfway up the stairs before he quit laughing. Holding it down to a mere chuckle, he called out, "Rudd told me that you're a psychologist. I was wondering if 'daft' is a professional term?"

I turned. "No," I growled. "The professional term for daft is the Latin, *non compos mentis*." Then I managed to flounce the rest of the way up the stairs and into Aunt Connie's apartment, slamming the door behind me.

I threw on jeans, sweatshirt, and hiking boots. As I went back downstairs, I decided that I was not at all amused by Mr. Freedom Crane.

"Where are we taking the body?" I asked as we took off down the alley in his beat-up old truck.

"I was out by Calley's Spring hunting for wood not long ago. Seems like that would be a good place."

"That's about five miles past Uncle Rudd and Aunt Nissa's farm. I used to go swimming at Calley's Spring in the summertime when I was a kid. Why there? Why not just run around the block a few times until Peggy leaves?"

"Because we don't know how long it will be before Peggy leaves, and we can't take the chance that she'll see us with Scott's body in the truck. Pink cellophane is pretty hard to miss. We don't want anyone else to see us, either. It would be safer just to take him out to the cave near the spring and leave him there all night. I figured we'd stop by Bender's Service Station and get some ice. Between the ice and the temperature in the cave, Scott's body will be okay until we can bring him back tomorrow. Then we can go back home and get some sleep."

"I know what cave you're talking about. In fact, everyone in the county knows about that cave! Not only is that spring a great swimming hole in the summer, it's the year-round make-out place for every teenager in a fifty-mile radius. Don't you think some teenager would either see us putting the body in the cave or find the body later on?"

Freedom shrugged. "It's Sunday, it's late, I think there is less chance of someone seeing us at the cave than driving around with a dead body in the back of the truck. Unless you've got a better idea, it's a chance we'll have to take."

The only better idea I could think of would be to drive right up to Sheriff Otis Beecher's house, knock on the door, and come clean. But it didn't look like that was going to happen anytime soon.

Up ahead I saw the large, well-lit sign advertising Bender's All Night Service Station and thought of a few other problems. "Aren't we going to have to get a lot of ice, and won't that look suspicious? And have you even thought about how we are going to find the cave, haul all that ice, and get Aaron's body in there?"

"I understand the problems. It probably won't be easy getting Scott's body and all the ice we're going to need into the cave. But as for getting the ice in the first place, that won't be a problem. The ice machine is on the side of the station, no reason for anyone to see us, and it's pay by the honor system. I'll just get what we need and stick the money in the jar."

I knew about the jar and Mr. Bender's honor system, but had forgotten about it. I asked Freedom how he knew about Bender's honor system policy with the ice.

"Rudd and I went fishing the other night and stopped here to get some ice for the coolers. Your uncle has been real good to show me around and make me feel welcome here in town."

Of course he has—we need new blood. Everyone else knows us and is afraid to get tangled up with the Tanner clan.

"You know, we'll be going right by Rudd and Nissa's place anyway, it might be a good idea to stop and get Rudd to help us out," Freedom said.

"Bad idea. They're asleep by now and have had enough turmoil." I certainly didn't want to encourage stopping by my aunt and uncle's. I had enough to deal with at the moment, and the last person I wanted to face was Uncle Rudd. Surely we could wait until morning to tell them. Besides, I was more worried about Aunt Connie and her state of mind. I wanted to get back to her apartment as soon as possible.

As we pulled into the station, I noticed that the youngest of the Bender sons was behind the counter. So much for Freedom and me looking suspicious. He never even looked up from the magazine he was reading as we drove by the plate glass window.

Freedom pulled up next to the ice machine and hopped out of the truck. I asked if he needed any help. He said no.

I stayed in the truck and took a good look at Freedom Crane as he crossed over to the ice machine. Not a bad-looking guy, actually. Dressed in a faded flannel shirt, jeans, and boots, along with that thatch of unruly salt-and-pepper hair and short beard, he looked more like a lumberjack than my conception of a big-time artist.

A few minutes later, he jumped back in the truck and started the engine. "Next stop, Calley's Spring."

I couldn't help myself. I had to ask how many sacks of ice he loaded in the back of the truck. I nearly cried when he said twenty. We were going to haul twenty sacks of ice and one dead body through a narrow pathway to a cave. It was going to be a long, long night. Just as we pulled into the dirt road entrance to the spring, my curiosity got the better of me. I had to ask. "Why are you doing this?"

He looked quite startled at the question. "I already told you, we couldn't let Peggy find out that we hid Scott's body in the flower cooler."

"No, I meant why did you get involved in this mess to begin with?"

"Oh, I see. It's not complicated." He shrugged. "I like your family. I was there. I wanted to help."

"Did it ever occur to you that if you really wanted to help

you would've talked my wayward relatives into going to the sheriff?"

"Nope," he said as he parked the truck and shut the engine off. Leaning forward he grabbed a flashlight out of the glove compartment then turned to me. "I'll go on up to the cave and look around, make sure no one is there." He flashed the light at his watch. "It's a little past ten. Let's hope no one is around this late. I've got a duffle bag in the bed of the truck. I think after I empty it out I can put several bags of ice in it, and I'll take that with me. You stay here until I get back."

Using the same words Aunt Connie used earlier, I snorted, "Fat chance."

We managed eight bags of ice in the duffle bag, and I carried three and the flashlight. We were relieved to see only one car off in the distance on our way to the cave. Freedom was right—it was downright chilly in the cave. We deposited the ice and went back for the body and the rest of the ice.

Back at the truck, we quickly refilled the duffle bag. Freedom hefted the body over his shoulder, and I grabbed the bag and led the way back to the cave. It was a good thing no one was around as we made our way toward the cave, because there was no hushing that infernal crackling sound of the pink cellophane.

By the time we had the body settled and packed in ice, my hands were numb and my whole body was shaking. We stood back and looked at our handiwork. Surely the man deserved better, even if he did leave my aunt at the altar. I hoped this nightmare would end soon and we could give Aaron Scott a decent burial. We took one last look, gathered up all the empty plastic bags, and made our way back to the truck.

Pulling out of Calley's Spring, Freedom again mentioned stopping at my aunt and uncle's house. I wanted to argue the point with him, but I couldn't dredge up enough emotional energy to say anything more than a whiney, "Can't we tell them in the morning?"

"We could," Freedom answered, "but I'll bet you anything Connie has already called Rudd and told him we had to move Scott's body. If we don't stop by, he'll be calling or coming over to Connie's anyway."

I hadn't thought of that. "Okay, but let's make it short and sweet. I don't want to leave Aunt Connie by herself for too long. And besides," I yawned, "I'm beat."

As we drove up I could see that the lights were burning brightly through the windows of the kitchen and the living room of the farmhouse. They also had the front porch light on, and both Uncle Rudd and Aunt Nissa were sitting together on the porch swing, wrapped in blankets.

We hadn't taken more than two steps away from the truck when both of them stood up and started talking at the same time. Aunt Nissa telling us she would bring out some coffee and Uncle Rudd wanting to know where we put Scott's body. Aunt Nissa shushed Uncle Rudd and told him to wait until she got some hot coffee down us. Good for Aunt Nissa. That's just what we needed.

By the time we settled on the porch, Aunt Nissa was back with cups and a pot of coffee on a tray.

I took a sip of my coffee and savored the warmth as I swallowed. I leaned my head back on the porch rocker and felt the tight muscles in my neck relax. I could've stayed in that moment forever. Uncle Rudd had other ideas. "Well, come on, out with it—where'd you put the body?"

I looked over at Freedom. "You tell him."

He did. Then I stared hard at my uncle. "He needs a proper burial, Uncle Rudd. We can't just wrap him up in pink cellophane and keep carting him all over the countryside, or leave him in the flower cooler much longer, either." I was quite definite on that point.

"I know, I know, I don't like doing this any better than you do." Uncle Rudd heaved a sigh. "But we're doing the best we can under the circumstances. We need us a clue awful bad, Dixie-gal. Did you find that blue note at Connie's place yet?"

Uncle Rudd was not a happy amateur detective when I told him no. For my part, I was not a happy put-upon niece when he lectured me on the importance of finding that note.

"Now, everyone is doing the best they can," Aunt Nissa interjected. "I'm sure Dixie will get ahold of that note as soon as she can." She stood up and started collecting our cups and stacking them on the tray. Looking at Uncle Rudd she said, "I think we've all had enough for tonight. Let them go on home, Rudd. Besides, we don't want Connie there alone much longer, now do we?"

Uncle Rudd dutifully stood up. "Guess you're right, Nissa. You kids need to get on back. We'll see you tomorrow." Aunt Nissa gave me a hug, Uncle Rudd shook Freedom's hand, and we left.

It was close to midnight when we got back to Aunt Connie's place. I was relieved to see the lights on in her apartment. She had waited up for us. After that lecture from Uncle Rudd, I was determined to find out about that blue note as soon as possible. And asking Aunt Connie about it was the quickest way I could think of to do it.

Freedom and I were both yawning as we got out of the truck and made our way to the stairway. At the foot of the stairs he stopped me. "Uh, Dixie, wait a minute. I just want to say that I know this wasn't the best way for us to meet. I'm sorry about that. Maybe after we both get some sleep, we can sort of start over tomorrow."

Our little foray into the wilds of Calley's Spring tonight did not bring any warm fuzzy feelings into my heart for Aunt Connie's new renter. I didn't want to start over. I had half a mind to just give him a curt nod good night, flounce upstairs, and slam the door on him, but the other half of me, the half that was trying to make some sort of sense of all this, said, "Look, I'm just curious, so don't give me some inane answer to a very simple question. Why did you and Uncle Rudd wrap that man up in pink cellophane?"

For a moment he stood there looking at me, the corners of his mouth twitching, then he said, "Well, Nissa thought he should have some sort of shroud, and she thought the pink stuff looked better than the green stuff."

"Oh, for crying out loud, you're all daft!" I huffed, and stomped up the stairs.

Just as I reached the porch I heard him say, "It's the truth, Dixie, honest, it's the truth!"

Thankfully, my aunt hadn't locked the door, so I was able to do a little flouncing and slamming after all.

Evidently Aunt Connie had dozed off while she was sitting on the couch. When I slammed the door, she woke up with a start and started flailing at the air with the long blue thing she was knitting. When she recognized me, she stopped. "Oh, Dixie, I'm glad you're back. Are you all right, child?"

"Yes, I'm all right." I was relieved that other than looking sleepy, she seemed as sharp as ever. "How did you and Peggy get along after we left? Do you think she really believed she must have mistaken that scarecrow for a dead body?"

Aunt Connie shrugged. "She didn't come right out and say it, but she's pretty sure one of us belongs in the loony bin, and it ain't her."

I flopped down on the couch next to her, untied my hiking boots, slipped them off, and curled my feet up under me. "After this escapade, we may all bypass the so-called 'loony bin' and end up in the so-called 'hoosegow.' By the way, how are you feeling after all of this?"

Although I was truly worried about my aunt's state of mind, I must admit my motives weren't entirely pure in asking her how she felt. There was the blue note issue to settle.

"If you mean am I about to have one of those episodes, I don't know. And if you mean how do I feel about Aaron's death, I don't know how well I'm doing in that category, either. I mean, after all these years, I never expected to see him again. It took me a good while, but I had made my peace with that. Then out of the blue he comes back to town, calls me, shows up here, and gets himself killed. I know it happened, but it doesn't seem real to me yet, so I don't know how I feel."

Aunt Connie sniffled and suddenly got up mumbling, "Excuse me," and went into the bathroom. I didn't try to follow her. I thought she probably needed a little privacy about now.

After a few minutes she came back with a bunch of tissues in her hand. Sitting down on the couch, she blew her nose, leaned toward me, and said, "Now listen, Dixie. I know Rudd is trying to do everything he can to protect me, even to the point of not letting me know everything that's going on with his investigation. I love him for it, but we almost got into a pack of trouble tonight. I never would've called

Peggy to come in if I had known where they hid Aaron's body. Whether Rudd likes it or not, I loved that man, and I intend to do the best I can to bring his killer to justice. To do that I need to know what's going on. So, as hard as it is for me to bear, I want to know where you put his body. Then we are going to put our heads together and see if we can come up with something that will help Rudd solve this thing. You understand me, Dixie June Tanner?"

CHAPTER SIX

Once I explained to Aunt Connie where we hid the body and why we picked the place we did, she smiled wistfully. "Aaron loved to explore caves. It was sort of a hobby with him. When we were courtin', we went out to Calley's Spring many times with a picnic basket. We would eat by the spring and stick our feet in the water. Then when we got tired of that, we would take our blanket and sit at the mouth of the cave and talk for hours. Dixie, you don't need to worry about putting him in that cave. He would have approved."

Then she sat up straight and briskly nodded her head. "'Course, it ain't whatcha call practical to keep him in the cave."

I nodded my head, too, like I understood the logic. Although it seemed to me that keeping a body in a flower cooler didn't qualify as practical either.

Aunt Connie acknowledged my nod. "I know we'll have to put Aaron back in the flower cooler. That's probably the safest place for him, so I gave Peggy the next five days off. She didn't want it at first, but when I sweetened the pot by giving her time off with pay, she finally agreed. So you and Freedom can bring Aaron back to the shop first thing in the morning. Now, what do you think we need to do next? Work on my memory or something like that?"

I took a deep breath. "Aunt Connie, I don't know why you're having what we now call episodes. I'm pretty sure you can't remember what happened because you were so traumatized. With time, the memory of that night will come back. But this afternoon, when you were up in the bedroom, you mentioned a blue note. Aunt Nissa had an idea that you might be referring to the note Aaron sent to you the day of the wedding, because it was written on blue paper. Do you still have it? I truly don't mean to cause you any more pain, but we think it might be important."

Aunt Connie gave a sad sigh. "Yes, I kept the note. I know what it says by heart, but if you think it might be important, I'll go get it and let you read it for yourself."

She went into her bedroom and came out a few minutes later with a yellowed envelope and handed it to me. I carefully took the note out of the envelope, opened the folded blue paper, and read what it said:

Dearest Connie,

If I could marry you today, I would.
Something has happened, and I have to leave town.
I don't think I can ever come back.
I'll always love you,

Aaron

I read the note once more, then carefully refolded it and put it back into its yellowed envelope. I handed it back to her and asked, "I know it's none of my business really, but what are your thoughts about why he left town so suddenly?"

Staring at the envelope, she said, "Certainly I've thought about it. I don't think he met someone else, although that's what most folks thought." She stopped talking and I saw the tears forming in her eyes. How painful that must have been for her, not only to lose the love of her life, but also to bear the rumors that must have been going around at the time.

She reached over to the side table where she had put her stash of tissues, grabbed one, and dabbed her eyes. "There was nothing I could ever think of that made any sense. Rudd always said Aaron seemed to be just fine at the bachelor party the night before."

This news about the bachelor party gave me the germ of an idea. If he wasn't a reluctant bridegroom that night, then something happened after the party and before the wedding. That narrowed the time frame we were looking at considerably.

I found myself asking Aunt Connie if I could use her phone to call Uncle Rudd. I only asked to be polite. I was already dialing the number by the time I finished asking.

After a mumbled and sleepy hello from Uncle Rudd, I got right to the point and told him I had the blue note and what it said. By the time I finished, he was wide awake.

Pressing on to the next point, I asked him, "Now, what

I need to know is, did anything funny, or out of place, or somehow different, happen at Aaron's bachelor party?"

"Not that I remember. It wasn't whatcha call a wild party or anything like that. We rented one of those little cabins on the lake and did a little fishing off the bank. That evening we sat around, ate fish, and talked. That's all."

"My, that was tame. You're sure no one snuck in a few beers to wash down that fish?"

"Dixie-gal, not a one of us had anything stronger than soda pop that night!" he boomed into the phone. "And you know good and well I don't hold with no drinkin'. None of us Tanners do."

It's true, the Tanner clan doesn't drink. We run from mildly eccentric to outright insane, but none of us drink. Go figure.

"Okay, but what about women? Any good-looking young girls jumping out of cakes?"

"Of course not!" he boomed again. "I told you, it wasn't one of those wild bachelor parties. Even if we had wanted to do that, which we didn't, Nissa and Connie had already put the kibosh on any girlie stuff. Me, Otis, and Dennis Reager were already married, Latham Sheffield was engaged. The rest might have had steady girlfriends, I don't remember. We weren't interested in that kind of stuff. We just wanted to catch some fish, fry 'em up, and have a good time."

"Simmer down, Uncle Rudd, you're going to wake up Aunt Nissa. I was doing a little fishing myself, only for information. However, that brings me to the next question.

Can you remember who all was at the bachelor party?"

"Well, if I can't, I'll wake Nissa up. Her memory is a sight better than mine. Let's see, I've already mentioned Latham Sheffield, Otis Beecher, and Dennis Reager. 'Course, there's me and Aaron." He hesitated a little before he said, "Oh yeah, it's coming back to me now. Truman Spencer was there. And Mitch Barker, Earl Standings, Daniel Martin, and Ed Baringer. I'm pretty sure that's it. I can check with Nissa in the morning."

"So there were ten of you there. No one acted funny. No hesitation from Aaron about the wedding?"

"No. Why? What's going on in that head of yours, Dixie-gal?"

"Well, since Aaron didn't seem to have any reservations about the wedding at the bachelor party, and nothing strange happened at the party, then that means something happened after the party and before the wedding."

Even though we were on the phone, I could almost feel the light dawning in Uncle Rudd's head. "Why, that's right smart thinking! That means not counting me and Aaron, we now have us eight suspects."

"I don't know about having any suspects, as you call them. You said everything was fine at the bachelor party."

"It was, as long as I was there."

"You mean you didn't stay the whole time?" That certainly put a whole new light on this suspect business. "When did you leave?"

"Whew, I haven't thought this closely about that bachelor party for years." I could hear him take a deep breath and let it out. "I think it was maybe ten, no later than eleven o'clock, when I headed out. I was the first one to leave, so I don't know how long the party went on."

"Didn't anyone say anything the next day about how you missed a good party and when it ended?"

"Dixie-gal, that next day all any of us had on our minds was that Aaron Scott left my baby sister standing at the altar all dressed in her fancy white wedding gown. No one cared about the bachelor party."

It was my turn to take a deep breath and let it out. "Okay, I'm convinced. Not including you and Aaron Scott, we have eight suspects." I turned to Aunt Connie and asked for a pen and some paper then said to Uncle Rudd, "Give me their names again. I'm going to write them down."

Once I had pen and paper, I wrote the names down and looked at them. "Uncle Rudd, I know everyone on this list except for this Earl Standings. Who is he?"

"He's a distant cousin of Aaron's. I know they grew up together. Come to think of it, he was the one who delivered the note and flowers. He said he found them in his car when he got in it to come to the church. Think that means anything?"

"Not that I know of. Listen, it's late, and all of us need some sleep. Tell you what, tomorrow I'll run over to the library and check the back issues of the newspaper around that time period. It's a long shot, but there might be an article that could throw some light on this. Maybe there was some mysterious happening that no one in the family caught because everyone was focused on Aunt Connie at the time."

"Now you're thinking like a real Tanner," Uncle Rudd gushed.

That struck me as a thoroughly frightening thought.

Just as soon as I put the phone down and started to get up off the couch, the phone rang again. Aunt Connie and I looked at each other. I reached over with a bit of trepidation and picked it up. "Hello?"

"Dixie-gal, I got one other thing to tell ya," Uncle Rudd informed me. "Before you go to the library, you need to go with Freedom to help him out with Scott's body. I'd do it, but I planned on taking apart that CJ-7 of yours to see if I can get it fixed for you. No sense putting too many miles on my Mustang. We'll come on over there around lunch and see if you've made any headway at the library. Nissa plans on us bringing some fried chicken and all the fixin's, so be sure and tell Connie. Oh, and tell Freedom he's invited to lunch also." He hesitated a moment then added, "Never mind about telling Freedom, I'll call him first thing in the morning and tell him our plan and invite him to lunch myself. Well, good night, sleep well." Then he hung up.

Oh yeah, I was going to sleep well. I had so much to look forward to.

Aunt Connie and I hugged each other and tottered off to our respective bedrooms. After I put my pajamas on, I didn't waste time with any nightly healthy-skin rituals. I just planted my tired bones on Aunt Connie's slightly lumpy guest bedroom mattress and fell asleep.

Lumpy mattress or not, it didn't stop me from having a vivid nightmare. In the nightmare it was my wedding day, but instead of a flowing white gown and veil, I was wrapped up head to toe in pink cellophane, and I had to be carried down the aisle. Everyone stood up and clapped, only they kept making this banging noise. I tried to make them stop, but they kept it up. Finally waking up, I realized that the people in my nightmare weren't clapping, someone was banging on Aunt Connie's door.

Aunt Connie came stumbling out of her bedroom at the same time I stumbled out of mine. I mumbled that I'd get the door. She nodded and veered toward the kitchen.

After tying my robe, I opened the door, and there stood a grim-looking Freedom Crane. "You and Connie had better get dressed and come on down to the flower shop. Somebody broke in there last night."

I started to push past Freedom, but he stopped me. "No, whoever was in there is gone now. It won't make a bit a difference if you take a few minutes to throw on some clothes before you come down. I'll go on back down and wait for you." With that he turned and went back down the stairs.

As Freedom's words began to sink in, Aunt Connie walked into the living room and asked what was going on. Judging from her reaction when I told her, she is not a morning person.

It was barely six, still dark outside, by the time we dressed and met Freedom down in the flower shop. Aunt Connie and I stood just inside the doorway and looked around. It struck me that it was an odd sort of burglary.

Everything had been neatly taken off the shelves and out of the cabinets. Clay flowerpots were all stacked, one on top of the other, in a corner. Next to the pots, bottles of flower shine and a various array of plant food containers were all lined up. Flowers and a few baskets were the only things strewn around the floor. Whoever broke into the shop was certainly a neat freak.

Freedom, standing near the opened flower cooler, nodded for us to look inside. Aunt Connie and I walked over and peeked in. Inside the cooler was the only real chaos. The now headless and mostly un-stuffed scarecrow lay at an odd angle on top of wads of pink cellophane.

I took a few steps into the front of the shop. Like the workshop, everything had been taken off of shelves and out of windows and placed neatly on the floor. Why? I thought I knew why the mangled scarecrow, but why take everything off the shelves? What was he looking for?

"Aunt Connie, you don't keep any money in the shop overnight, do you?"

Coming over to stand next to me, she shook her head and said, "Never have. If I can't make a night deposit, I keep it upstairs in my safe, so they couldn't have taken money—there wasn't any. Nothing seems to be missing. What were they after?"

"I think whoever was in here was looking for Aaron's body, Aunt Connie."

"What!" Aunt Connie's eyes widened and her mouth dropped. "You mean the killer came back to the scene of the crime? What would the killer want with Aaron's body?"

Leaning on the door frame between the workshop and the storefront, Freedom answered, "I think Dixie's right about the killer looking for Scott's body. My guess is that since you didn't get framed for his murder, the killer is now driving himself crazy trying to figure out why the body hasn't surfaced yet. Which makes him a very dangerous person right about now."

"But if he was looking for Aaron, why take all the stuff off the shelves and stack it all so neatly on the floor? Was he afraid we would hear him?" Aunt Connie asked.

"As long as I'm guessing," Freedom said, "I'd say that once he couldn't find the body, he took all that stuff off the shelves looking for the cutting shears he stabbed Aaron with. Maybe he was careful about it because he was trying to be quiet. He certainly took some anger out on that scarecrow. Doesn't make a lot of sense that he would be so careful about where he put stuff then rip that scarecrow to shreds, but then murder isn't a sensible act."

"Where are the cutting shears?" I asked.

Freedom shrugged. "Rudd took the shears with him when he took Nissa and Connie home. I don't know what he did with them after that."

Aunt Connie waved an exasperated hand in the air. "I guess there's no tellin' what that murderin' thief was thinkin', so there's no sense in worryin' over it. Right now we got enough problems. We have to get this place cleaned up and put back together before it's time to open up the shop."

I grabbed her arm before she could even move a step. "Aunt Connie, what we need to do right now is call the sheriff and tell him about the break-in."

Before I could state my case any further, Freedom countered with, "Or we could call Rudd and let him know what happened."

The opportunity to debate the issue was settled by the tall, lanky form of Sheriff Otis Beecher standing in the doorway to the workshop.

With his hand resting lightly on his gun, Otis let out a low whistle. "Well, I'll be! This is the second break-in we've had in less than five months. But this seems a might different than a couple of kids breaking into Hattie Goodwin's cellar to steal a few apples."

I was shocked to see him. Between that and guilt, I was surprised I could speak. "Otis, how did you get here so fast? We haven't even called you yet, and I know Aunt Connie doesn't have an alarm system."

Otis shrugged, ducked his head, and walked on into the workroom. "Just making my regular rounds. I pulled into the alley, saw the door open and the lights on back here, and thought I'd better check it out." Looking directly at Aunt

Connie, he added, "And if you and the other shopkeepers around here would put in alarm systems like I been askin' you to at every shopkeepers' meeting for the past several years, I might've been able to catch this thief red-handed."

"Too expensive." Aunt Connie folded her arms across her chest and stared defiantly back at Otis.

"Yeah, I've heard that argument umpteen times," Otis replied. Then he looked at his watch, took a pen and pad out of his front shirt pocket, and mumbled out loud, "Official time of report, 6:18 a.m." Then he looked up at us. "Okay, I need to ask the three of you some questions. Did anyone see or hear anything suspicious last night or early this morning?"

All three of us answered no. We were the only ones around that we knew of who were acting suspicious.

"All right, when and which one of you discovered the burglary?"

"Not too long before you walked in, maybe thirty or forty minutes ago," Freedom answered. "I got up around five this morning to do some work on one of my wood sculptures. When I went into the kitchen to make a pot of coffee, I didn't have enough to make a pot, so I decided to run down to Bender's and pick some up, and maybe a Danish or two for breakfast. When I came downstairs I noticed the door was open. At first I thought maybe Connie was up, but when I walked in, I found it like this. I went upstairs and woke Connie and Dixie up. They came downstairs, and then you came."

Otis looked thoughtful for a moment, said, "Excuse me," and went back outside. When he came back he had a clipboard in his hand. "This is the schedule for what time we make our rounds this week. I vary it from week to week so no one can figure out where my deputy and I will be at any given time. Take tonight, for instance. Billy made rounds at one o'clock this morning. He reported that he ran Dozer Moss in for drunk and disorderly, but everything else was quiet. I started my rounds at five thirty."

"So you're saying the burglar had to come sometime after one and before five thirty this morning," said a voice with a nasal twang, coming from behind where we were all standing.

All of us turned around to find Truman Spencer, the owner/editor of the Kenna Springs *Bugle* standing in the doorway.

Truman bears an uncanny resemblance to a frog. His eyes almost pop out of his head, and he has a thin-lipped, extra-wide mouth. His head looks like it spent its formative years in a vice grip, and when he walks, his stocky body sort of hunches over.

"Truman! What are you doing here?" Otis grumped.

Holding his flat little nose in the air, Truman answered, "I happen to have the nose of a reporter. After all, I am an editor and a journalist."

"That still doesn't explain what you're doing here at this hour of the morning," Otis said.

"All right, since you asked. As you should know by now, I am an early riser, as any newspaperman should be. I was driving by on my way to my office and noticed your patrol car parked in the alley. Thinking there might be a story, I stopped and came on in."

There was something wrong with Truman's story, but I couldn't quite put my finger on it.

Before I could figure it out, Truman had the audacity to pull out his own notepad and pen and ask Otis, "So, do you think you might have any leads at this time on who could've burglarized the Red Carnations Flower Shop?"

Otis frowned. "What I think, Truman, is that you oughta get in your car and find somebody else to be bothering. I'm not about to answer any questions until I complete my investigation. Now, if you don't want to see it that way, then I'll give you a little incentive. I can call my deputy right now and have him haul you down to the jailhouse for obstructing justice. 'Course, at the moment, only one cell has the new plumbing finished, so we'd have to put you in with old Dozer Moss. And right about now Dozer's got himself one head-bashin' hangover going on. Like as not he won't feel like having any company around to irritate him. I imagine you could get in some pretty good exercise tryin' to keep away from him."

"Otis, sometimes you can be an impossibly crude human being." Truman huffed as he fumbled with the lapels of his tweed jacket. "But since you are the sheriff of our fair city, and hold the hammer of justice, as it were, I will have to defer to your judgment. However, I would like to stop by your office this afternoon and pick up what crumbs of information you might be willing to throw my way."

Then without an ounce of surprise at my presence, Truman nodded at me. "Miss Dixie, nice to see you back in town."

He turned slowly to Aunt Connie. "I want you to know that I am very glad that you are unharmed. If I may, I would like to interview you. At your earliest convenience, of course."

Aunt Connie gave him one of her beady-eyed stares. "I know it won't do a bit of good to say no. You'll just keep pestering me till I give in, so we'll make it easy on both of us. Come back later on today."

He gave Aunt Connie a stranger than usual widemouthed smile, then he left.

When I heard Truman's car door slam shut, it dawned on me what had been wrong about what he said to Otis. The route Truman Spencer would have to take from his home to the newspaper office does not go by Aunt Connie's alleyway. I felt my stomach lurch. Maybe he had a good explanation, maybe not. For the time being I would have to file that piece of information away. Otis was asking us questions again, and Deputy Billy had just arrived with a camera and the equipment he needed to get fingerprints.

"You made good time, Billy," Otis said. "I appreciate that. Go ahead and take pictures before you start lifting prints."

Otis turned back to the three of us. "I radioed him when I went out to get the clipboard."

Billy worked quietly, snapping pictures with his camera while Otis asked questions, wondered out loud about the torn-asunder scarecrow, and generally poked around the shop. It took more than an hour to determine that nothing had been stolen. Of course, any one of the three of us could have told him that.

Eventually, Billy got around to fingerprinting us. He told us that it would at least eliminate some of the multitude of differing prints around the shop. Other than a practice session on how to lift prints, Billy didn't seem to think anything useful would come of his efforts.

Finally, Otis flipped his notepad shut and put it back in his front shirt pocket. Taking one last look around, he sighed. "It sure beats me if I can figure out what the thief or thieves wanted when they broke in here. Especially since you didn't have so much as fifty cents worth of change lying around. Only thing I can figure is they must've thought it was an easy target and took the chance you didn't make a night deposit. Which means they must be plumb stupid or from out of town."

Otis was wrong on both counts. The person who broke into Aunt Connie's shop was murderously intelligent, and he was somewhere right under our noses.

After Otis and Billy left, Aunt Connie looked at her watch and groaned. "It's almost time to open up the shop. You all straighten up the front." She grabbed the phone with one hand and waved us out of the way with the other, adding, "I'll take care of the workshop and call Rudd and let him know what's going on. You kids go on now. I still have to make a living, you know."

"Been a long time since someone called me a kid." Freedom grinned.

"Me, too," I said, grinning back. "And we'd better get to work, or she might take a switch to us." Both of us laughed, and for a moment I marginally liked Mr. Freedom Crane. Or at least I didn't dislike him as much as I had.

Since our thief/more likely murderer had been impeccably neat, it didn't take us long to put the flower arrangements back in place, stuff the bins with the silk greenery and flowers, and put Aunt Connie's fall arrangements back in the display windows.

Aunt Connie was stuffing what was left of the scarecrow and the wadded-up pink cellophane into a plastic trash bag when we walked back into the workshop.

"Here, let me finish that and take it out to the trash bin for you," Freedom offered.

Aunt Connie handed him the sack then said to me, "Before I forget, and lately I've been doing a lot of that, I talked to Rudd, and he thinks it might be a good idea if you went on down to the library."

"I thought Uncle Rudd wanted us to go get the body and

bring it back here first. We can't just leave him in that cave!" Not that putting him back in the flower cooler was such a great idea, but it was better than the cave.

Aunt Connie shrugged. "Plans have changed, I guess. Rudd wants you to get on down to the library and check out that stuff you talked about last night."

"What about helping you to get the flower shop ready to open?"

"For cryin' out loud, Dixie June, if you keep flappin' that jaw of yours, none of us will get anything done. We've just about got the place back in order, anyway. Freedom can help me with what's left. You go on down to the library. It'll be opening up soon, but you got time to grab you some breakfast upstairs before you go." Then taking a sharp look at me, she added, "And while you're at it, comb that hair and put on some makeup before you go out in public."

With that piece of advice I went upstairs to do what she said, even sneaking in a quick shower. After I dressed, I sucked down a glass of orange juice, crammed a couple of graham crackers in my mouth, called it breakfast, and left.

The library was just off the town square, about two blocks from the flower shop. I could walk it. There is nothing like fall in the Ozarks. The morning air was cool and the brisk breeze across my face felt good. I took a deep breath and felt like I could run for miles and jump any and every fence that happened to get in my way. It was a heady feeling, and

I wished I could stay in that moment for a long, long time. But reality has a way of rearing its ugly head, and the reality was that I wasn't out for just a pleasant walk.

CHAPTER SEVEN

The Kenna Springs Public Library hadn't changed much, except maybe there was a little more ivy covering the gray stone walls. The place had always looked more like a medieval castle than a library. And in this castle there lived a dragon.

Head Dragon Lady, Acantha Fry, stood behind the main desk with her chin jutting out, her deep-set eyes watching as I approached.

I told myself that I now have a career as a clinical psychologist. I've taught assertiveness training classes. I've come face-to-face with exactly two paranoid schizophrenics. I graduated at the head of my self-defense class—which I enrolled in right after meeting my second paranoid schizophrenic. Surely, I was much too experienced to be intimidated by Acantha Fry. Then I watched her lips stretching out over her huge teeth, slowly bending upward into what passes for a smile, and I thought, maybe not.

Looking me up and down, she smacked her lips. "Well, well, Dixie Tanner. Have you suddenly discovered an affinity for libraries, or is there something else I can help you with?"

"Me? Uh, well, no, not an affinity really. Not that I don't like libraries. I just haven't been to the library lately. I mean, this library specifically, but I go to the one in Little Rock. I live there now, you know. Not in the library, but in Little Rock, in a townhouse. . ." I stammered, stuttered, rambled, and may have even drooled a little bit for all I know.

It was all I could do not to start rummaging through my wallet until I found my Little Rock library card to show her. I had to get hold of myself.

"Look," I said with a little more confidence, "I'm here to do a little research on a. . .well. . .a project." Then doing a little subtraction in my head, I told her, "I need to use the library computer to look at the Kenna Springs *Bugle* for 1965."

"Computers!" She nearly spit the word out of her mouth. Then crossing both arms over her meager chest, she said, "They are in the back of the library. Not that microfilm wasn't good enough. I'll go back with you and help you get set up."

She led the way and I followed. Over her shoulder she asked, "What month and date do you want in 1965?"

She had me there. I could figure out the year on my own, but I had forgotten to ask anyone about the date of the wedding. I quickly announced, "The whole year, of course," figuring once I got settled at the computer, I could use my cell phone to call and get the date.

Miss Fry's arched eyebrows went almost all the way up to her graying widow's peak. "All right. I assume you are familiar with computers?"

I assured her that I was.

We reached the computers. I had my pick of any of the three terminals. Miss Fry pulled up the *Bugle* for the year I wanted, gave me a quick lesson on going from month to month, and left me alone.

I still needed to know the date of the wedding. I called the flower shop and got hold of Aunt Nissa. She couldn't remember the exact date, but knew it was in June. Close enough.

In 1965 the *Bugle* was a bimonthly, so I only had two newspapers to look through in June. I read the first one from cover to cover—nothing. As I pulled up the second newspaper, a hand came down on my shoulder. I did what anyone with my nervous system would do. I squealed, loudly.

Before I got a chance to turn around and see who had come up behind me, I saw Dragon Lady barreling toward me with a fierce and fiery look on her face.

"It's okay, Acantha, I just came up behind my niece and startled her," I heard Uncle Rudd say.

Dragon Lady stopped in her tracks, gave us both a withering look, turned around, and headed back to her lair.

With my heart still rapidly thumping from the scare, I whispered to Uncle Rudd, "You almost got us kicked out of the library. What are you doing here?"

"Sorry," Uncle Rudd said and pulled up a chair to sit next to me. "I got your Jeep fixed, but came on over to Connie's in Nissa's car. After we helped Connie get opened up, Nissa went ahead and drove the Mustang home. She'll drive your Jeep back. I came on down here to see if you found anything yet."

"Not yet, but I'm just getting ready to start on the second newspaper."

He got his glasses out of his shirt pocket and put them on then leaned forward. "Okay, let's divide up the reading and it will go quicker."

"That's not going to work," I whispered back. "The screen's too small. Go walk around, pick out a book. Just do something."

"I am doing something. I'm helping you."

I might as well have been asking a stack of books to amaze and entertain everybody by throwing themselves off the shelves and doing an Irish jig.

All of a sudden Uncle Rudd tapped his finger on the screen. "THAT'S IT!" he yelled. "WHAW HOO! I BET THAT'S IT, DIXIE-GAL!"

The Head Dragon Lady lost no time steamrolling her way toward us. Before I could even shush Uncle Rudd, she was right beside him.

"Rudd Tanner! You old coot," she said in a hoarse whisper. "You do that again and I'll grab one of your earlobes and escort you right out of this library!"

"Old coot! Who're you callin' an old coot, Acantha Fry?" Uncle Rudd stood up and faced the Dragon Lady. "I would like to remind you that we are the same age. I remember when you were just a stick of a kid. And I'll be hanged if I let you drag me out of here by my earlobe!"

Miss Fry crossed her arms and stood her ground. "I warn you, Rudd Tanner. I've thrown bigger and younger men than you out of my library."

They stood there, face-to-face, glaring at each other. I kept shifting my gaze from one to the other, waiting.

Uncle Rudd was the first to make a move. It started as just a flicker around his mouth. Then there was a low sort of gurgle, then a sputter, and when he could no longer contain it, he laughed. He laughed. . .very long and very loud.

My gaze shifted to the Dragon Lady. Her eyes widened, her mouth dropped, and she stood perfectly still and stared.

Uncle Rudd took a handkerchief out of his back pocket and wiped his eyes. "Acantha, I haven't laughed this much in a good while. I must admit, I didn't know you had that kind of stuff in you. I guess if you're that set on throwing me out, I'll leave on my own."

"Maybe Uncle Rudd could wait for me by the front door. I need to run off a copy of this article, then we'll be through here, anyway." I looked at the Dragon Lady. "If that's okay with you?"

Keeping her eyes focused on Uncle Rudd, she gave a

curt nod. "All right, Dixie, but make it fast. And no more outbursts from you, Rudd Tanner, you hear me? This is a library, not a zoo."

It was Uncle Rudd's turn to nod, and we both watched Dragon Lady amble off.

My uncle looked at me and grinned. "Imagine getting thrown out of a library at my age. I'd appreciate, though, if you didn't mention this little incident to Nissa. You know how she is. She'll complain she won't be able to hold her head up in town." He walked off toward the entrance.

I ran off the copy. I didn't take time to read it—just grabbed it out of the printer, folded it, and paid Miss Fry for the copy. I met Uncle Rudd at the front of the library.

As soon as we were outside, I unfolded the article with the headline, WOMAN MISSING, and started to read it. But before I could read more than a sentence, Uncle Rudd snatched it out of my hands. "What are you doing waving that around in public? The killer could be watching us right now."

"Don't you think that's just a little paranoid?"

"No, I don't," he grumped. "I don't even think we should be talking about it right now." He handed back the article. "Here, put it in your purse. You can read it later."

I resigned myself to wait. "Did you walk down here, or drive?"

"I walked. I may be an old coot, but I can still make it quite a ways on my own steam, thank you."

"If you can't, I know someone back at the library who

would be more than willing to toss you every bit as far as she could throw you, and by your earlobe, no less." We both laughed.

For the next few minutes we strolled down the sidewalk and talked about normal stuff, like the new bull, the price of cattle, and whether or not Aunt Nissa would actually use a dishwasher if they had one put in. I loved it.

As we walked past Patsy's Café, Uncle Rudd changed the subject. "Uh, Dixie-gal, you notice that the weather today is warming up pretty good for October?"

"Yeah, I guess it is warmer than usual for fall." I smiled back, because I still thought we were talking about normal stuff.

"Uh, well, we need to talk about that. . .the uh, weather, I mean."

"But we just did. What else is there to say?"

Uncle Rudd looked down at his shoes and started pulling at his lower lip. Clearing his throat, he pitched his voice low and spoke fast, "The weatherman on the radio said we could expect above-normal temperatures for the next few days. Supposed to get near seventy degrees today."

Looking at what must have been a blank on my face, Uncle Rudd leaned even closer and spoke out the side of his mouth, "Dixie-gal, don't make me spell it out. I know you ain't dumb. Connect the dots. Heat, melting ice, cave, Connie's cooler. . ."

In my defense, I hadn't connected the dots right away

because I'm not in the habit of referring to dead bodies in the course of normal conversations. In fact, I try very hard not to refer to them at all.

"Oh. . .yeah. . .I get it," I muttered.

Both of us picked up our walking pace. Under the circumstances, the quicker we got back to the flower shop, the better.

"Let's go through the front rather than around to the alleyway. It'll be quicker." Uncle Rudd motioned to the door a few feet away. I put my hand in my purse and got hold of the copy of the newspaper article, planning to read it as soon as we entered the shop. I was burning with curiosity to find out just who the missing woman was and whether she could possibly have had anything to do with the murder of Aaron Scott.

The first sound we heard after we walked through the front door was the nasal twang of Truman Spencer. Disappointed, I took my hand off the article and left it in my purse.

Uncle Rudd frowned at him. "Truman," he bellowed, "if I find out you've been harassing my baby sister, I'll squeeze your stumpy little neck until it's no thicker than a string bean."

"Now, you listen here, Rudd," Aunt Connie groused, shaking her finger at him. "I don't need you to be pullin' any of that big brother stuff for me. If Truman gets out of hand, I'll be the one to squeeze his stumpy little neck."

Truman held a protective hand up to his throat. "You

Tanners have always been an assertive lot, but this is quite over the top, isn't it?"

"SHUT UP, TRUMAN!" Aunt Connie and Uncle Rudd yelled at the same time, still glaring at each other.

I plopped my purse down on the workbench. "Okay, that's enough out of you two!" I pitched my voice a little louder than my relatives. "No one will be squeezing anyone's neck around here."

I had the satisfaction of watching both my aunt's and my uncle's mouths drop open. Pressing what little advantage I had, I walked over and stood next to Truman. As gently as I could, I said, "Look, Truman, this probably isn't the best time for you to hang around. Do you think you have enough information for the paper?"

"Yes. . .yes, of course," Truman stammered, keeping an eye on Aunt Connie and Uncle Rudd. "That's all I was trying to do, you know, just gather the information I need for the paper. It's my job." Holding his hands up in the air like he was surrendering, Truman started moving sideways past Uncle Rudd. "I'm through here. I'll just go on back to the office now."

Once past Uncle Rudd, Truman turned around and caught his elbow on my purse, knocking it off the workbench. He was too startled to catch the purse, and no one else was close enough. We stood there watching as it hit the ground, spilled open, and splattered its contents all over the linoleum floor.

Mumbling he was sorry, Truman bent down to retrieve all the odds and ends now littering the floor.

Uncle Rudd and I lunged toward the one thing we didn't want him to see, the newspaper article. But Truman got to it first.

"What's this?" Truman asked.

Snatching it out of his hand, I quickly answered, "Just some research I'm doing. I'll get the rest of it picked up, Truman. I'm sure you're in a hurry to leave." I rolled my eyes toward Uncle Rudd for emphasis.

Following the direction of my eyes, Truman nodded. "Uh, yes, I guess I'd better go. Sorry about your purse, Dixie." He gave me an odd look and left the flower shop.

Uncle Rudd watched him leave then turned to me. "Do you think he got a look at that article?"

"Maybe the headline," I said.

Uncle Rudd shook his head. "Well, couldn't be helped. No real harm done, I guess." Then he turned and asked Aunt Connie, "What'd he want?"

"Wanted information about the break-in." Aunt Connie shrugged. "He was here earlier this morning asking about it, but Otis ran him off. I told him to come back later. He came back later."

It was at that moment I remembered what Truman said earlier, and I asked Aunt Connie, "Did Truman ask you anything about Aaron?"

"Just said he'd heard Aaron was back in town and asked

me if I'd seen him. He didn't make a big deal out of it."

Uncle Rudd looked alarmed. "What'd you tell him?"

Placing both hands on her hips, she let us have it. "I want you two to know that I'm still a sight smarter than that potted plant Dyson talks to all day. I told Mr. Nosy Spencer that it was none of his business. So, just what do you two worry warts think of that!"

"I think you did just fine." Uncle Rudd chuckled.

"I think you did just fine," I echoed. "Because the less Truman Spencer knows the better off we'll be. It's bad enough if he saw that headline. After all, he's a prime suspect."

"Dixie-gal, I'd be the first one to tell you that I don't have much use for the man, mainly because Truman's got it into his head that he's a cut above the rest of us. But, murder! Why would you think Truman's our killer?"

Aunt Connie nodded in agreement with my uncle. "Truman's stuck on himself, but that don't make him a killer."

"I didn't say that I thought he did it for sure," I said. "I just think he's a prime suspect. Look, just hear me out. For one thing, he was at the bachelor party. That automatically puts him on the list. Then this morning, he told Otis that he just happened to be on his way to the newspaper office when he saw the police car parked in the alley, and in the so-called interest of journalism, he stops to see what's going on."

I shut up and waited for them to put two and two together. Judging from the blank stares, they were coming up with a grand total of zero.

"Don't you get it? Truman lives on the other side of town. His newspaper office is on the other side of town also." I pointed and waved my hand in the direction of his home and office.

Their faces still registered zero.

"Oh, for crying out loud. Unless the man is stupid enough to circle the entire town square, he doesn't drive by the flower shop on his way to work, and that's what he told Otis he did."

Finally! It registered.

Aunt Connie looked up at Uncle Rudd. "I do remember Truman telling Otis that."

Uncle Rudd took a deep breath and let it out. "Have to admit, it's a little odd that he would say that. On the other hand, he could have a good explanation. Maybe he was on some sort of errand that took him near here."

"Why wouldn't he just say, 'I was on an errand and drove by the shop'?" I asked.

"I dunno." Uncle Rudd shrugged his shoulders almost up to his jaws. "He just might've, I guess. Look, you may be right. Truth is, I don't know if he's the killer or not, but if he is, we may be in a pack of trouble if he saw that headline on the article."

"Maybe we should read it right now," I suggested, pulling the article back out of my purse and spreading it out flat on the worktable.

Uncle Rudd nodded then looked at his watch. "Let's wait a few more minutes. Nissa should be back any time now." He looked around the room. "Where's Freedom? He'll want in on this, too."

"He's upstairs," Aunt Connie told him. "After you left for the library, I sent him back to his place to take a nap. That boy was tuckered out. Rudd, you go wake him up and tell him to come on down. I'll go upstairs with you and get the food Nissa sent over. When Nissa comes we can eat lunch down here and go over that article you keep talking about. Dixie June, no fair reading it without us."

I almost groaned out loud with frustration. I was pretty sure that real detectives wouldn't have to wait for fried chicken, potato salad, one aunt, and a sleeping sidekick.

In an effort to keep my sanity, I reached into my purse and pulled out my cell phone. "Since we're waiting, I think I'll check in with my secretary and see how things are going at the clinic."

Estelle Biggs was just the person I needed to talk to right now. Always cool and always calm, that's Estelle. In fact, I looked forward to talking to her. She answered on the second ring.

CHAPTER EIGHT

"Hi Estelle. How are things at the office? Who did you find to take care of my clients?"

I waited for her to answer, but there was nothing more than dead air on the line.

"Estelle? Can you hear me?" I thought maybe we had a bad connection.

"I can hear you. I am trying to decide how to phrase my reply."

I knew that couldn't be good. "Have you decided?"

"Yes, I've decided. I got ahold of Dr. Gaitherman, and he is seeing your clients for the rest of this week." Estelle enunciated each word and spoke more slowly than she usually does.

This was not going to be an easy conversation. I gathered my quickly diminishing supply of false bravado. "I'm glad he was available. So, how are things going then?"

"The answer is that they are not going well at all. At the moment, Mr. Woodbine is hiding in the coat closet in your office, refusing to come out."

"I see. Well, actually no, I don't see. Why is Mr. Woodbine in my coat closet?"

"Because he is afraid," Estelle answered.

"Estelle, Mr. Woodbine is afraid of roughly 87 percent of the known world. That's why he's in therapy. Could you be more specific?"

"Maybe it would be best if you spoke to Dr. Gaitherman. Would you like for me to get him on the line?"

Yes, I would, but before I could say anything, Aunt Connie walked into the shop, followed by Aunt Nissa and Freedom, along with Uncle Rudd carrying a picnic basket and a large jar of iced tea. I could either talk to Dr. Gaitherman or I could read the article.

"Estelle, I don't have time to talk to him right now. Tell Dr. Gaitherman that I think he can get Mr. Woodbine out of the coat closet if he will take one of the candy bars out of the stash I keep in my desk and offer it to him. Mr. Woodbine is not afraid of candy. I once got him out from under my desk that way. Try it and see. I have to go now. I'll call you back as soon as I can. Good-bye."

Before anyone could chomp into a piece of Aunt Nissa's fried chicken and I had to wait any longer, I said, "Let's read that article right now before we eat lunch."

We gathered around the workbench where I had spread out the article earlier. Realizing it was a tight squeeze for the five of us to read it together, I grabbed the article and read it out loud.

The report was short and not so sweet. The missing woman's name was Dolly O'Connell. She was from Brogan's Ferry. Dolly went missing the same night as the bachelor party. Her boyfriend, Chad Gunther, reported her missing two days later. Clothes and luggage were missing from her apartment. Even though they found her car a few miles from Addison's Mill, the conclusion was that Dolly had simply run off and there was no foul play, so they called off the search.

"I can see why this article piqued your interest, Uncle Rudd," I said. "Do you think Aaron ran off with this woman, and that's why he left town? Surely that wouldn't get him murdered."

"Aaron didn't run off with no Dolly what's-her-name," Aunt Connie exploded. "He wouldn't do that! I know he wouldn't."

"Simmer down, Little Sis. I don't think that's it at all. I do remember that some of the guys at Aaron's bachelor party were talking about a woman named Dolly. Seemed like the talk was that she was sort of fast and loose, if you know what I mean. But I'd never met her and didn't know who she was. I got the impression that Aaron didn't know her, either."

"Told you so." Aunt Connie crossed her arms across her chest and looked directly at me.

"But everyone else knew her?" Freedom asked.

Uncle Rudd thought a moment then nodded. "Near's I can remember, most everyone else had either heard of her or knew her."

"So, if I follow you," Freedom said, "you're thinking that one of these guys at the bachelor party murdered Dolly. Somehow Aaron found out about it, or maybe saw it, someone threatened him, and he was scared enough to leave town. Then when Aaron comes back into town, the murderer gets spooked, follows him, and kills him?"

Uncle Rudd nodded. "That's about the size of it."

"That certainly makes sense, except that it's true we still don't know why or if Dolly was murdered, or who did it," Aunt Nissa interjected.

"I know Aaron loved me." Aunt Connie spoke the words so softly that all four of us turned to look at her and saw the tears flowing down her cheeks. "He told me the truth. He didn't have a choice, he had to leave town. He was trying to protect me."

I put my arms around her and let her cry on my shoulder. There was nothing for any of us to say. This was Aunt Connie's time, her moment of bittersweet memories. After all these years, she had some closure. What she didn't have was Aaron Scott.

Aunt Nissa reached in her purse and handed Aunt Connie a tissue. She dabbed her eyes and blew her nose. Taking a deep breath, she looked at each of us in turn. "I'll be okay. It's just that after all this time. . .well, I need to get ahold of myself. There will be plenty of time to grieve later. We got to find the one that killed my Aaron." She looked directly at Uncle Rudd. "I just wish all this hadn't happened the way it did."

"Baby Sister, I want you to know that even though Aaron Scott wasn't high on my list of favorite people, for your sake, it don't bring me any joy that he's dead."

"I know that, Rudd." She dabbed her eyes one more time then straightened her shoulders and put on a brave face. "So, what's our next move?"

Uncle Rudd pulled on his lower lip for a bit. "Okay, here's the thing. We got to figure out if anyone was going to see Dolly after the bachelor party that night. I'm not sure just how to go about that. I'll have to think on that awhile. But in the meantime, Dixie-gal, you go with Freedom and bring Scott's body back here. Whoever killed him has already checked this place out, so his body should be safe here for the time being. And as long as the killer doesn't know where it is, we're safe. In the meantime, the three of us will figure out a way to go snooping around for the information we need. How's that sound to everybody?"

I didn't know about "everybody," but I would rather not run around the countryside lugging around dead men. Been there, done that. But from the look on Uncle Rudd's face, I knew I didn't have much of a choice in the matter.

"Seeing that no one's got any objections," Uncle Rudd said, "it's settled then. You two better grab you some chicken to eat on the way."

Surprising all of us, Aunt Connie piped up and said, "Wait just a minute, Rudd. I got something to say 'bout this plan of yours."

Uncle Rudd barely got the words "you do" out of his mouth.

"I certainly do! Did it ever occur to any of you that Aaron probably intended to stay around town for more than a day? If he did, he had to check into a room somewhere." Aunt Connie looked very proud of herself as she stood there with her hands on her hips, tapping her little foot, encased in the latest style of orthopedic footwear, on the linoleum flooring.

That really was good thinking on her part. I could see the possible problem. "Uh-oh, you're thinking that if he doesn't come back to pick up his luggage or pay his bill, then someone's going to call the sheriff. And of course, you would be one of the first people Otis would want to question!"

Now it was Aunt Connie's turn to look surprised. "Oh, well, no, that's not what I was thinking at all. Although, I'll be sure to worry about that now that you mentioned it, young lady! I was thinking more along the lines that maybe we could get into his room and rummage through his luggage for any clues."

All of us stood there and stared at each other. With ten or fifteen years of training, we might make it to amateur detective status.

Freedom broke the silence. "While it would be nice if we could get ahold of Scott's luggage, Dixie has a good point. It's likely he did check into a room somewhere, and somebody is bound to get suspicious that he hasn't come back. The most logical place for him to check into would be Tance's Bed and Breakfast. Anything else would be too far out of town. The easiest way to find out is for Rudd or Connie to call over to Tance's and ask for Aaron Scott and see what they say. Then we'll have a better idea of what we might be dealing with."

Uncle Rudd answered, "I think maybe Freedom is right. We'd better call the bed and breakfast and see if we can find out anything."

"You do it, Rudd," Aunt Connie pleaded. "The number is on that sheet taped on the wall by the phone."

Uncle Rudd nodded and started toward the phone.

It was nerveracking for all of us to wait. Aunt Connie grabbed my hand and held it tight in both of hers. Freedom paced back and forth. Aunt Nissa picked imaginary lint off her sweater.

Finally Uncle Rudd hung up the phone. Turning to us with a huge smile on his face, he said, "I talked to Tance. We're okay!"

Aunt Connie flashed Uncle Rudd a toothy grin and demanded a blow-by-blow account of his conversation with Tance Laribee.

"Okay, the upshot of this thing is that Scott did check into Laribee's late Friday night, around midnight. He didn't call ahead, he just got Tance out of bed. She said if this wasn't her off-season and she didn't need the money, she never would have answered the door that late at night. She didn't recognize him at first, but when he told her who he was, she asked what he was doing back in town. He told her he was here to settle something and try to get back what he lost. He had one suitcase and a briefcase with him. He paid his bill Saturday morning, but the strange thing was that he asked her to hold a room for him. He said that if all went well he would be back late that night; if not, he wouldn't. He took his luggage with him. She told him there was no rush on rooms, it wouldn't be a problem. She said he never came back; 'course, we know why."

I wondered out loud why Aaron would settle his bill but reserve a room for that night.

"I don't know the answer to that one, Dixie-gal. Like I said, that is the strange thing. Maybe he thought if things worked out with Connie, he'd stay. If not, he'd leave."

"Did Scott drive into town?" Freedom asked.

Uncle Rudd snapped his fingers. "Oh yeah, almost forgot about that! Tance said that he told her he came in on the bus."

One other thing occurred to me. "Uncle Rudd, you said that Tance told you that Aaron took his luggage with him. What did he do with it when he came over here to see Aunt Connie?"

After a short discussion, we could only surmise that either Aaron hadn't brought his luggage and briefcase, in which case we had no idea where those things were, or the killer took them with him. Either way it seemed to be a moot point for us.

"Okay, there's nothing we can do about Aaron's stuff, but we're still safe, for the time being, anyway. As it turned out, it's a good thing Peggy saw Aaron and you had to move his body. Otherwise whoever murdered him would have found it. We still have the body and the upper hand, so let's get back on track here." Uncle Rudd reached over and grabbed a plate out of the picnic basket and started putting pieces of fried chicken on it. "Freedom, you and Dixie take this with you to eat on the way to the cave. I know it's not much of a lunch, but it'll have to do for now."

Five minutes later, I found myself sitting in Freedom's truck with the plate of chicken between us. I tried to tell myself that I should be too stressed, too frustrated, and too civilized to eat chicken while on my way to pick up a dead body wrapped in pink cellophane. But the truth was that the orange juice and graham crackers I had for breakfast were just a memory, and I was hungry.

Freedom must have been hungry also, because other than a few appreciative yum-yum sounds, neither of us spoke as we munched on our chicken.

Once my stomach was satisfied, I didn't want to continue to sit in silence. It was time to find out about Mr. Freedom Crane.

"What made you move all the way from California to Kenna Springs? Do you have relatives around here or something?"

Tossing the bone from a chicken leg back onto the plate

between us, he answered, "I guess I don't mind telling you the answers to those questions. Are you sure you want to hear them?"

"Why not?" I shrugged.

Looking at the road ahead, he nodded. "Okay. I left California because after my wife died, it no longer seemed like home, and I needed a new start."

That was not what I had expected. All I could do was murmur an inadequate, "I'm sorry you lost your wife."

Turning toward me, he said, "Don't get me wrong, Dixie, I'm not asking for your sympathy. I'm giving you the answer to your question. I realize I'm sort of the new guy on the block, and you have a right to know as much about me as the rest of them do. Do you still want to hear my story?"

I nodded. For maybe the first time I was seeing Freedom Crane as a real person—a person, who like all of us, struggles with life and death.

"Okay." Freedom nodded back and turned to look at the road. "Abby died seven years ago in a car accident. We were married only two years. A drunk driver hit us. I was in the hospital for months. Abby died instantly. When I got out of the hospital, my body was fine, but I was a wreck mentally and emotionally. Anger was the only thing I could feel for a while. I hated the guy that ran into us, especially when I found out that he only suffered a few broken bones. As far as I was concerned, he should have died a slow and agonizing death for what he did. Prison wasn't good enough. I was even angry at Abby for dying on me. Most of all I was angry at God. Up until the accident I didn't believe God existed. Then I wanted Him to exist so I could be angry with Him. Just before she died, Abby came to believe in God. She believed the Bible. She believed that Jesus was her Savior. Jesus was very real to her. But from what I could see, He hadn't saved Abby from dying, so what good was He?"

Freedom turned his head again to look at me. There was pain in his eyes. And because I saw his pain, there was pain in my own heart for him. I couldn't trust myself to say anything. I could only hope that he saw what he needed to see in my face.

Freedom turned again toward the road ahead. "For almost five years that anger nearly ate me alive. I couldn't get rid of it, I couldn't deal with it. One night, I was eating at a diner near where I lived at the time, and a van pulled up. The logo plastered on the side of the van was from some seminary close by. Seven guys piled out of the van. I watched them, hating them, as they walked through the door of the diner. One of the guys was a lot older than the rest. I thought maybe he was a teacher or something like that, and I decided I wanted to talk to that guy. I wanted to tell him how unfair I thought God was. I went up to him and told him I saw the logo on the van and wondered if I could talk to him. I was very polite about it, because I wanted him to think he had a patsy for his religion. We went back to my table. The short version is we had quite a discussion. No matter what I said, the man was unflappable. He had this peace about him that I just couldn't penetrate. After a while, I ran out of steam and started listening. We made plans to meet again. It turned out he wasn't a teacher. He was a seminary student studying to be a preacher. We became friends and started eating together once a week at the diner."

We had reached the turnoff to Calley's Spring and Freedom stopped talking. He pulled into the clearing, stopped the truck, and turned toward me. "My friend got me interested in a Bible study, sort of a Christianity 101. Through that study, I came to see Jesus like Abby saw Him. I saw that Jesus was everything Abby said He was. So, I traded my anger for forgiveness and peace and became a Christian. Haven't looked back since. It brings me comfort knowing that I'll see Abby again. My friend not only pointed me in the right direction spiritually, he was the one who suggested that if I was set on moving, to try out Kenna Springs."

"Your friend suggested Kenna Springs? Why?" The words popped right out of my mouth.

I saw the corners of Freedom's mouth twitching into a grin, "As it turns out, he happens to be related to you. He's a second or third cousin, I think. Goes by the name of Woody."

"Woody Tanner! Hang 'em high, let him swing from the neck, Woody Tanner is studying to become a preacher?" I just couldn't believe it. "But Woody left town years ago. His parents moved down to Florida before my parents did. No one that I know of has ever heard from him. Does Uncle Rudd know this?"

"Yep, you bet he does!" Freedom made it sound like an announcement. "He knows the whole story and has even talked to Woody. When I met Woody two years ago he hadn't been in seminary very long. He didn't want to get in touch with his family just then, because he wanted to be able to prove to them that he had changed. He's ready now, and in fact, as we speak he's in Florida visiting with his mom and dad and I guess your mom and dad as well."

Freedom sat quietly, giving me time to absorb everything he had told me. I appreciated that, because my mind was in a whirl. Woody Tanner a preacher. . .a changed man! I would have to get used to that concept. I found myself. . . well. . .happy for Woody. Stealing a glance out the corner of my eye, I decided that I had changed my mind about Freedom also. He wasn't quite as crazy as I once thought.

Breaking the silence, I murmured, "That's quite a story." I wanted to say more. But everything I thought about saying seemed too mushy, too gushy, too trite. I settled for, "Thanks for being honest with me and answering my questions. But it seems to me that you came all the way from California just to land in the outskirts of insanity with the rest of us Tanners."

"You may be right." Freedom grinned, opening up the door on his side of the truck. "But we'd better get to that cave so we can get Scott's body back to the shop. No telling what those three will be up to by the time we get back."

He had a point. We looked around to make sure there

were no other vehicles or people in sight, and headed down the narrow dirt path toward the cave. At least it was daylight and didn't take as long to get there. Freedom was able to weave his way in and out of the brush and trees. All I had to do was stay right behind.

We decided to leave as little evidence as we could. Using Freedom's coat as a carrier, we cleared away any ice that hadn't melted and threw it in the brush. There was nothing we could do about the puddles of water on the ground and on the ledge around Aaron's body, except hope they dried up quickly. When we were done, Freedom hefted the cellophane-wrapped body over his shoulder, and we headed back to the truck.

CHAPTER NINE

Freedom backed the truck down the alley behind the flower shop to make it easier to get Aaron's body back into the flower cooler. He turned off the engine and we got out of the truck just as Uncle Rudd, Aunt Nissa, and Aunt Connie came out of the upstairs apartment.

"We've been watchin' for ya," Uncle Rudd said, leading the pack down the stairway. "Any trouble?"

"No trouble, just took longer than we thought it would," Freedom told him.

Freedom pulled the tailgate of his truck down and started to pull Aaron's cellophane-wrapped body toward him.

"Here, let me help with that," Uncle Rudd offered and moved to take the other end of the body.

They hadn't taken more than two or three steps when the wet cellophane slipped through Uncle Rudd's fingers. With the shift in body weight, the cellophane slipped through Freedom's hands as well, and the body went crashing to the ground.

"Oh, for crying out loud!" Uncle Rudd bellowed, and

actually stomped his foot.

The three of us women scrambled toward Uncle Rudd and Freedom to help. We all grabbed a section of the pink cellophane and were ready to lift the body when we heard, "Does Maybelle hear someone a yellin' out of anger on the Lord's day?"

All five of us looked up and saw Maybelle Chesewick standing over us.

Maybelle always spoke about herself in the third person. She is the closest thing Kenna Springs has to a bag lady, although Maybelle isn't actually homeless. She lives in a small frame house just off the town square. She isn't actually penniless either. She owns nearly a thousand acres of good farming land, which she leases out. What Maybelle is, is a woman who lives in her own little world and is content with that. She walks up and down streets and alleyways with her battered shopping cart and picks up everything from banjos to plastic pink flamingos. As long as it is outside, not nailed down, and she can fit it into her shopping cart, Maybelle considers it hers. If anyone really wants anything back, she is not opposed to bartering. More than one person in town has shown up at Maybelle's house with a casserole or some other bartering material in hand to get back whatever she took.

This was not a good time for Maybelle Chesewick to show up. But there she was, standing there frowning, with her bright red woolen cap covering her head, and an orange sweater over her royal blue sweatshirt, which didn't even begin to match her bright turquoise blue knit leggings.

Aunt Nissa thought quicker than the rest of us. She stepped over Aaron's body and stood in front of it. The rest of us took our cue and did the same, instinctively closing ranks.

"Now, Maybelle, Rudd wasn't yelling out of anger, exactly," Aunt Nissa said soothingly. "And really, Maybelle, this isn't the Lord's day. It's Monday, dear."

Maybelle shook a crooked finger at Aunt Nissa. "Maybelle knows that, you dunce! Don't matter the name of the day, every day is the Lord's day, and Rudd should'na yelled like that. That's what Maybelle thinks."

Then she bent down so that she could peer between our legs. "Whatcha got there?"

Aunt Connie bent down to look into Maybelle's face. "Ain't nothin' you need to concern yourself with, Maybelle. It's just somethin' that needs to go in the flower cooler."

"But Maybelle wants to see what's wrapped in the pretty pink paper." She straightened and sniffed, rubbing her nose with her gloved hand.

"Maybelle, get it through that spooky little brain of yours there ain't nothin' wrapped in that cellophane you need to be lookin' at," Aunt Connie snapped. "Besides, what's in there wouldn't fit in your cart, and you wouldn't know what to do with it if you had it anyway."

Fearing that might be too much information, I intervened, "You know, Maybelle, maybe I could walk through the alley with you, and we could spot something pretty you might like to put in your cart."

Maybelle cocked her head and squinted her eyes to get a better look at me. Her eyes lit up, and she smiled. "Maybelle knows you. You're Dixie, Memphis and Jeb's daughter. Maybelle likes Memphis and Jeb. They were always nice to Maybelle." Shooting a quick glance at Aunt Connie, Maybelle added, "Not like some Tanners I know."

"So, you'd like to take a walk with me down the alley, Maybelle?"

Tilting her head first to one side, then the other, Maybelle said, "Well. . .maybe. Maybelle already found a real pretty leather thing by the trash cans over there by the door early yesterday morning."

It flashed through my mind that she might have found Aaron's briefcase. Unfortunately, before I could ask, Aunt Connie gruffly demanded, "Just what kind of stuff did you find around here yesterday, Maybelle Chesewick?"

Looking about as far from being intimidated as one could get, Maybelle narrowed her little eyes and announced, "Maybelle never talks to mean people."

Trying to sound as casual as I could, I smiled at her. "Maybelle, if you still have it, could I see the leather thing you picked up by the trash cans yesterday morning?"

Maybelle knit her almost nonexistent brows together, evidently to think about it before she answered. "Well. . . guess it can't hurt none to show you."

She walked over to her cart and started taking things out and dropping them on the ground. When she got to the bottom of the cart, she pulled out a brown leather briefcase. Holding it so we could all see it, she ran one of her hands over the dark leather. “Pretty, ain’t it?”

Without thinking, I reached for the briefcase. Maybelle jumped back a step and yelled, “No, it’s Maybelle’s!” Then, wrapping her arms around the briefcase and pulling it close to her chest, she glared at me. “Doesn’t belong to you! Maybelle found it fair and square.”

Aunt Nissa said gently, “Maybelle dear, we think that briefcase is important to us. Could we barter for it?”

Maybelle smiled slyly. “Can Maybelle see what’s all wrapped up in that pretty pink paper?”

When the four us heard Aunt Nissa say, “Of course, dear, if that’s what you really want,” there was a collective gasp that could be heard two blocks away. Then she added, “But I think I have something you might like a little better than taking a peek at some of Connie’s old stuff.” At that, the four of us let out all that air we had sucked into our lungs.

Aunt Nissa quickly took off her earrings and held them out to Maybelle. “See, I’m wearing the same glittery earrings you admired a couple of weeks ago. I’ll trade you these earrings for the briefcase.”

Maybelle’s eyes widened. “Ohhhh, Maybelle likes those earrings.”

“Dear, they’re only colored glass. But if you like them, I

would certainly be willing to take the briefcase for them."

Pink cellophane all but forgotten, Maybelle made the trade. Once that was done and Maybelle's cart was reloaded, we waved her a cheery good-bye, and all five of us beat it into the workshop to see what was inside the briefcase.

Aunt Connie locked the door behind us and let out a big sigh. "There! We don't want anyone busting in on us." She looked at Freedom. "Go pull that curtain between the workshop and the store closed. The bell at the front door will ring if anyone comes in."

While Aunt Connie and Freedom were busy securing the workshop, Uncle Rudd was busy hugging Aunt Nissa. "Honey bunch, you are one smart little lady. First thing I'm gonna do right after we save Connie from going to jail is buy you another pair of earrings. This time the real deal, not just colored glass." Then he gave Aunt Nissa a big ol' kiss right on the lips!

Rolling her eyes, Aunt Connie intervened. "Well, I'm just as giddy as a baby vulture circling roadkill that you two can still ogle each other like two teenagers, but if we're gonna keep me outta jail, we need to get that briefcase open."

With that largely unsentimental comment, Aunt Connie grabbed the briefcase from Aunt Nissa's hand and plopped it on the workbench. The rest of us crowded around her, nearly butting heads in the process. Aunt Connie had just placed her hands in position to unlatch the briefcase, when Freedom startled us all with, "Wait a minute, we left Scott's body out in the alley!"

I don't know about anybody else, but I felt just out-and-out stupid. How were we ever going to solve this crime if we couldn't keep track of the victim?

Without a word, we filed out of the workshop, gathered around the body, and grabbed hold of as much pink cellophane as we could get. When Uncle Rudd said, "Heft!" we carefully and respectfully picked the body up and carried it into the workshop. We laid him on the side rack of the flower cooler and shut the door. By silent consent we agreed not to discuss the incident.

Looking at each of us in turn, Uncle Rudd gave a curt nod. "Okay, back to the briefcase."

With our enthusiasm dampened somewhat, we crowded around the workbench. Aunt Connie tried the latch. It wouldn't budge.

"Let me try," Freedom said, reaching into his pants pocket and pulling out his pocketknife.

It didn't take him long to trip the locks and open the briefcase. One quick look at all the stuff in the briefcase and the incident in the alley, while not quite forgotten, no longer distracted us.

It was everyone for themselves. Each of us reached in and grabbed something. While I'm not proud of it, I must say that I was one of the worst. I nearly knocked Aunt Connie over getting an arm through the mob to grab something. She got even though by stepping on my foot. In a matter of seconds each of us had something from the briefcase.

We were all talking at once when Uncle Rudd called a halt to the pandemonium. "All right, everybody, calm down. We can pool our information better if we each take a turn and tell the others what we found." Then he pointed at me. "You go first, Dixie-gal."

I was already flipping through the checkbook I had in my hand to see what information I could find. "The address on his checkbook says he lives in Fort Walton Beach, Florida. Oh my! That's not far from where Mom and Dad live in Destin! But the name on the checks is Landon Scott. Why Landon Scott?"

"Because Landon is Aaron's middle name," Aunt Connie informed us. "He never liked the name Landon. I don't know why he would use it."

"Maybe because he was afraid to go by Aaron," Freedom answered. "Check his bank balance, Dixie, see if there is anything out of the ordinary there."

I flipped back to the register. When I saw the balance I felt my eyes popping. "Well, Aaron Landon Scott was not a poor man. In fact, if this checkbook is any indication, he's fairly well-off. The deposits look pretty normal in the sense that they are made at regular intervals for about the same amounts each time. I wonder what he did for a living?"

"I have the answer to that one." Aunt Nissa held up a business card case in one hand and a business card in the other. "He owns a marina and rents boat slips. His business card says: Landon's Landing, Boat Marina, then gives an address and a phone number to call for rental fees and availability."

"Owns a marina! Aaron around boats?" Aunt Connie grabbed the card out of Aunt Nissa's hand. "I can't hardly believe that! When we were together, Aaron loved to fish from the bank, but no one could get him into a boat. Said it made his stomach queasy and his head spin." Aunt Connie stared at the business card and shook her head. "Wonder why he decided to buy a marina, of all things?"

"Even if he didn't like boats, he wouldn't necessarily have to get on the boats," I said. "All he had to do was to rent the slips for other people's boats."

"I think he was covering his bases," Freedom said. "Just like using his middle name instead of his first name. Being around boats might have seemed safe to him, if whoever he was running from knew that he wasn't crazy about boats."

"Smart man," Aunt Nissa said.

"Always was," Aunt Connie added.

I thought maybe with this information we could narrow the suspects a bit. I turned to Uncle Rudd. "Who was at that bachelor party that would know Aaron well enough to know he didn't like to go out on boats?"

"Everybody knew Aaron didn't like to go out on boats. We fished off the bank at the party because he refused to go out fishing in Latham Sheffield's boat. None of us were too happy about that, I can tell you. Latham had a real nice boat he kept docked only a mile or so away from the cabin we rented that night. If Aaron hadn't been the bridegroom-to-be, we would've left him standin' on the bank and gone on Latham's fancy boat."

"That's no help then." I groaned. "Anybody else got anything?"

"I found a one-way bus ticket to Kenna Springs from Fort Walton Beach and a funny-looking little key," Aunt Connie said, peering into a white letter-size envelope. "Think that's any help?"

Uncle Rudd asked to see the key. Turning it over in his hand several times, he finally said, "You know, I think. . ."

Before Uncle Rudd could tell us what he thought, he was interrupted by the loud jangling noise of the bell over the front door. Someone had come into the flower shop. Although whoever it was couldn't see us because of the curtain between the workshop and the front, we acted like we had just been caught with our hands in the cookie jar. We threw whatever we had in our hands back into the briefcase. Uncle Rudd shut the lid on the case and quickly pulled some wrapping paper over it. When everything was put up and covered, Aunt Connie took off for the front of the shop.

"Oh dear, what if it's Otis?" Aunt Nissa fretted.

Giving me a none-too-gentle shove in the direction of the showroom, Uncle Rudd told me to go on out and see if Aunt Connie needed any help. Once through the curtain into the front of the shop I saw that it was Latham Sheffield. Relieved that it was the tall, lanky owner of Jobina's Jams and

Jellies and not the extra-tall, lanky sheriff, I pasted a smile on my face and greeted him.

"Hello, Dixie, good to see you again." Then, turning to Aunt Connie, Latham said, "I heard about the break-in. News travels fast in this town, as you know. Are you ladies doing all right? Must have been pretty scary."

"We're all right," Aunt Connie said. "More mad than scared. Mighty nice of you to ask though."

Latham leaned on the counter, took a toothpick out of his pocket and put it in his mouth, then shook his head slowly. "Just could hardly believe it when I heard it. Otis got any leads on who might've done it?"

"Not a one that I know of," Aunt Connie answered.

Latham looked down at the counter and rolled the toothpick around in his mouth for a moment. "Uh, I hate to bring this up, considering what you've been through today, but did you know that some people are saying that Aaron Scott is in town?"

I saw Aunt Connie's back stiffen. "I know."

"Oh, then you've seen him." This time Latham looked up and smiled at Aunt Connie like she had just told him he'd won a free vacation to the Caribbean.

"I. . .uh. . .I haven't talked to him face-to-face, if that's what you mean," Aunt Connie stammered.

He dropped the smile for a frown. "I'm not trying to be nosy, really. I was just wondering if you'd seen him lately. Just wanted to say hi to him, before, well, before. . ."

"Who told you Aaron Scott was in town, Latham?" I asked, to give the poor man time to get his foot out of his mouth, and because I was curious about how he got the news.

Looking relieved, Latham answered, "Ah, well, let's see, I believe it was Truman."

Aunt Connie cleared her throat and said, "I hate to hurry you along here, but I got some work to do in back. Did you come in to get Barbara some flowers? I have some real pretty deep red roses I could fix up for you."

"Roses. Oh. . .no, I think I'm supposed to pick up some flower arrangements for something Barb has going on tomorrow."

"Either you haven't talked to your wife lately, or else you haven't been listening real good when she's been talking," Connie teased. "Barb picked up those flower arrangements first thing this morning."

Apparently Latham didn't get the joke, because he defended himself by barking back, "I'll have you know that I talk to my wife every day, and I assure you I listen to every word she says!" Then looking rather sheepish, he added, "I thought I was supposed to pick up the flowers. Guess not."

It was a good try on Aunt Connie's part, but Latham Sheffield has always been the intense, overly serious sort, and had never been known for his sense of humor.

After Latham left, Aunt Connie commented that she bet he did listen to his wife, since it was her money that

Latham used to expand the plant several years ago. Then she looked at me, winked, and we both turned to go back into the workshop.

We hadn't taken more than two steps when the bell to the front door jingled again, and this time it was Otis Beecher, sheriff's badge and all.

CHAPTER TEN

Otis greeted us with, "Afternoon, ladies. I was on the way to the station to relieve Billy for his dinner break and thought I'd check in on you. I wondered if you found anything missing since we talked this morning."

At least he was smiling. I felt like my tongue was glued to the roof of my mouth and only managed a weak smile back. Maybe it was just my guilty conscience at not telling Otis about Aaron Scott, or maybe it was just outright fear we were all headed for jail, but whatever kept my mouth shut did not seem to affect Aunt Connie.

"Nope, nothin' else that I can tell. And other than being a little rattled, we're doing all right." Then, like an old chum settling down for a long chat, Aunt Connie leaned on the other side of the counter from Otis. "But what gets me about this whole mess is that whoever broke into my place was mighty persnickety about taking stuff off those shelves and such."

Aunt Connie's comment not only surprised me, it scared me. Had she forgotten that her ex-fiancé's body was in the flower cooler? The last thing we needed was for Otis to start exploring other options besides burglary for the break-in.

Frowning, Otis replied, "Been wondering 'bout that myself. Somethin' sure doesn't seem right about it. It almost looks like the burglar was lookin' for something specific. I can't see what that would be in a flower shop, though. Truth is, we don't have a lot to go on. Well, ladies, I'd better go so Billy can get some supper. I'll keep you posted on anything I find out." With that, Otis put his hat on and walked out the door.

Aunt Connie looked at her watch. "It's almost five o'clock. I think I'll just close up shop a little early. Then we can get back to that briefcase uninterrupted."

Uncle Rudd poked his head through the curtain again. "All clear?"

"All clear. I've locked up for the night," Aunt Connie told him.

As we started toward the workshop, Uncle Rudd walked out from behind the dividing curtain and blocked my path. Holding up his hands in front of him, he said, "I know you've already had a pretty full day, Dixie-gal, but I've got one more little job for you and Freedom."

The last thing I wanted to do was to go on one of Uncle Rudd's "little jobs." My mind was shot, I was hungry, I was tired, and I wanted to eat and sleep, not necessarily in that order.

Reluctantly and slowly I said through clenched teeth,

"What little job?"

My tone of voice and whatever awful look I had on my face made Uncle Rudd take a step back and blink. "Let's go on back into the workshop, and we can talk about it."

I followed Uncle Rudd back through the curtain muttering phrases like, "Sleep would be nice," "A trip to the Bahamas would be better," and, "This better be important."

Uncle Rudd heard that last comment and turned around to face me. "It is real important, Dixie-gal." Then he started digging in his front shirt pocket and brought out the small key that Aunt Connie had found in the white envelope in Aaron's briefcase. He held it in the palm of his hand toward me. "I think this key is one of those locker keys down at the bus station. Since Scott came in on the bus, we figured he went back there and rented one of those lockers to store his suitcase in. All you and Freedom need to do is to go down there and pick it up."

"Can't we go check on the locker tomorrow? It's been a long hard day already." I literally whined.

"You could, except you and Freedom need to go over to Brogan's Ferry first thing tomorrow morning."

I barely kept myself from snarling like a wild dog. "And why are we going over to Brogan's Ferry tomorrow morning?"

"Now, Dixie-gal." Uncle Rudd started to pat me on the shoulder then thought better of that idea. "While you and Freedom were bringing Scott back, I got to thinking about Chad Gunther, Dolly's boyfriend. I knew I'd heard that name connected with some sort of business that had to do with cars. I got out the phone book and poked around in the yellow pages. Sure enough, Chad Gunther owns an auto repair shop. The plan is for Nissa to help Connie in the shop tomorrow, and I'm goin' ta pay a visit to some of the guys that were out at the bachelor party. You know, talk about old times, see what comes up. That leaves Chad Gunther for you and Freedom."

Uncle Rudd pleaded with his eyes, holding out the small key for me to take.

"Okay, but Freedom doesn't have to go with me to the bus station. Surely I can manage to pick up one piece of luggage by myself."

"Dixie-gal." Uncle Rudd shook his head. "We're all tired. I figure two tired heads are better than one tired head if something comes up."

"I don't mind going," Freedom offered.

There wasn't any use in arguing. I grabbed the key and we headed out. I insisted we take my Jeep. At the moment I needed every little bit of control I could get.

The bus depot in Kenna Springs consisted of a ticket counter, two straight-backed benches, a soda machine, and a candy machine, along with several battered gray lockers standing against one wall. The walls needed painting and the green and white swirled tile floor was beyond polishing.

Except for Fog Whitman, who was reading a book and manning the ticket counter, no one was inside the depot when we walked in.

Freedom and I matched the number on the key with the number on one of the lockers. I put the key in. It fit perfectly, but wouldn't open the door. Another keyhole in the door told me that the lockers were set up to use two keys. Presumably one was a master key.

There was nothing else we could do except get the other key. Fog was so engrossed in his reading he didn't pay any attention to us when we walked up to the counter. When he didn't acknowledge us after a minute or so, I cleared my throat to get his attention.

Fog carefully laid a bookmark on the page he had been reading and put the book aside. Just as carefully, he patted the thin, gray sprigs of hair on his head then brought out a black, well-worn, official-looking hat from underneath the counter and plopped it on his head. "I see you, Miss Dixie. No need to be in some all-fired rush. There ain't another bus leavin' here for another two hours. You got plenty of time. 'Course, nothin' says you can't buy you a ticket in advance. Goin' back to Little Rock, are you?"

"No, Fog, I'm not going back to Little Rock just yet. I wanted to talk to you about something else, if you don't mind."

"Company rules say to be polite, but no social visits. Sorry, Miss Dixie. Been a company man for thirty years. I know the rules. Next!"

I turned my head to see if someone had walked in behind

us. “Fog, no one else is here.”

“Who’s he, then?” Fog pointed at Freedom.

“I’m with her.” Freedom pointed at me.

“Look, Fog, we need some help with the lockers.” I kept a smile on my face. “You’re the man to see about that, aren’t you?”

“Yes,” Fog answered slowly, rubbing his bottom lip with his thumb. “ ’Course, those lockers are officially for them that have bus tickets, so I couldn’t let you use one of them lockers. Unless, of course, you want to buy a ticket.”

There was nothing to do but persevere. “Fog, listen carefully. A man named Aaron Scott came in on the bus a couple of days ago. Do you remember Aaron Scott?”

“Don’t know if he did or he didn’t. I don’t recall knowin’ any Aaron Scott.” As far as Fog was concerned, the conversation was over. He picked up the book, opened it, and began reading.

It might have been a bit much to assume Fog would remember a man that hadn’t been in town for four decades. On the other hand, surely Fog had heard the talk going around back then about Aunt Connie and Aaron Scott. Maybe he just needed me to jog his memory a bit.

I cleared my throat again to get his attention. “Pardon me for interrupting, but this is important. Aaron Scott was the man who was engaged to marry my aunt, Connie Tanner, about forty-some-odd years ago. Does that ring a bell?”

Fog scrunched up his bird-like face to ponder the question.

"No, can't say as it does. You mean to tell me that this fella and Connie are just now gettin' hitched? My, them folks is mighty slow. Longest betrothin' time I ever heard of before this was a couple down in Wolf Summit. But they was waitin' on his mother to pass away."

I mentally counted to ten then said, "Fog, what I am trying to tell you is that a man named Aaron Scott came in last Friday on a bus. We know this man. He left some luggage in one of the bus depot lockers. We have the one key." I held up the key to show Fog. "We need the other key from you to get the stuff out of his locker."

Fog pushed his glasses up on his nose, leaned forward, and slowly looked the key over. "Yep, that's one of ours. If that key belonged to that Aaron Scott fella, then he's the only one that's authorized to use it. I can't give you the other key because you ain't Aaron Scott."

"I told you, Fog, we know Aaron Scott," I said through clenched teeth.

"Do you have somethin' in writin' authorizin' you to pick up his things? Otherwise, I don't know how you came by that key. Most folks just take their luggage with 'em when they come in to town. How come this fellow didn't do that?"

Raising my voice, I growled, "No, I don't have anything in writing! I don't know why Aaron didn't take his luggage with him. Maybe it clashed with his plaid suit for all I know. The point is we need to get his stuff out of that locker, and to do that we need the other key. Surely other people have come in and picked up other people's stuff out of those lockers without a note."

"Nope," was all Fog said, and it infuriated me. Without thought, just raw emotion, I slapped both hands on the ticket counter and yelled, "FOG WHITMAN! YOU FORK OVER THAT KEY THIS MINUTE, OR I'M COMING IN THERE TO GET IT!"

Fog reached up with one hand and yanked on the rolling louvered screen above him. It rumbled down between us and snapped shut.

"You got no call to talk to me like that, Miss Dixie," Fog called from the other side of the screen.

"Fog Whitman, you little chicken." I started pounding on the screen separating us. "You open up this screen immediately! You hear me?"

"That's against the rules, Miss Dixie," Fog squeaked back.

"Rules! I'll show you rules!" I climbed onto the counter and banged on that stupid screen as hard and as loud as I could.

"Dixie! Dixie! That's enough!" Freedom caught me by the waist and swung me around behind him. "Calm down. Let me try to talk to him."

"Have at it," I told him, and threw myself down on one of the nearby benches. I'd had all I could stand of Fog Whitman.

Freedom knocked softly on the screen and called Fog's

name. "It's me, the man that came in with Dixie. Remember? My name is Freedom Crane. Dixie doesn't really mean you any harm. She's just uptight about some family problems right now. You can come out now, Fog, it's safe. I won't let her hurt you."

The screen came up about five inches and Fog peeked through. "If you don't mind my sayin' so, Miss Dixie, you might be in need of some sort of counseling."

"I am a counselor!" I snapped back, and Fog slammed the screen shut.

Freedom held his finger to his lips in a motion for me to keep my mouth shut, then he knocked on the screen again. "Fog, you'd like for Dixie to leave wouldn't you? She'll leave if you just give me the other key that goes with that locker. How about it, Fog?"

There was a moment of silence, then a quivering voice said, "Maybe that's best under the circumstances, Mr. Crane." The screen lifted just far enough for Fog to shove the key we needed out to where Freedom could get to it, then the screen slammed shut. In the same quivering voice, Fog added, "Please leave the master key on the counter when you leave, and don't forget to take Miss Dixie with you."

Freedom took both keys and went over to Scott's locker while I stayed on the bench. With my anger spent, I was now rather busy feeling humiliated. I just couldn't believe I had acted that way. I was tired, yes. I was stressed, oh yes. But I had been tired and stressed before and hadn't acted like that! Of course I had never spent a day quite like this one in my life. I had the distinct thought that had my ancestor Tenacious Tanner been here he would have understood. And that sent chills down my spine.

Standing in front of me, Freedom held up one medium-sized, tan-colored suitcase. "That's it?" I asked. Not much to show for my childish display.

Freedom nodded. "That's it."

He put the suitcase down next to me and walked over to the still-closed screen. Knocking gently on it then turning to wink at me, Freedom said, "Fog, I left the other key in the locker, and I'm putting your master key on the counter. Give us a minute or two and we'll be out of your hair. Thanks."

"Mr. Crane, is Miss Dixie a goin' with you?" Fog asked.

"She sure is, Fog," Freedom answered.

"Thank you, Mr. Crane," Fog squeaked from behind the screen.

As we walked out, Freedom put his arm around me and gave my shoulder a sympathetic squeeze. We got into the Jeep and drove to Aunt Connie's flower shop in silence.

The savory smell of Aunt Nissa's chicken and dumplings hit me as I walked into Aunt Connie's apartment. Even that couldn't tempt me. I was no longer hungry, just tired and thoroughly disgusted with myself.

Uncle Rudd, in quite a chipper mood, decided that the suitcase could wait until after we ate our supper. I found myself being gently but firmly steered toward a seat at the table by Freedom. Aunt Nissa filled our plates, mentioned apple pie, and Uncle Rudd said grace. I forced myself to take a bite. After all, I was going to need all the strength I could muster to continue my pity party. I found I was hungry, ravenous in fact.

Between bites, Uncle Rudd asked, "Have any problems getting that suitcase?"

I stopped in mid-bite and looked over at Freedom, pleading with my eyes for him not to tell them how I'd badgered poor old Fog Whitman.

Freedom looked at me with laughing eyes and grinning mouth. "We were having quite a bit of trouble convincing Fog we needed his master key, but you should have seen your niece in action. . ."

By the time Freedom finished telling everyone my wild-woman saga, we were all laughing, including me. As I listened and watched his face as he told the story, I found that I was grateful to him. He managed to take some of the sting out of my humiliation. He really wasn't a bad sort, and he was a good storyteller to boot!

When Freedom had told it all, Uncle Rudd beamed at me and lifted his iced tea glass up in a toast. "Dixie-gal, you've just had a lesson in being human. May you take this opportunity to glean from it all that the good Lord has to teach you. There's hope for you yet!"

I had certainly learned that I needed to let the Lord teach me about patience. Something I thought I had until I came up against Fog Whitman. I looked at each one sitting around the table, and I realized that the love and laughter of family and friends had brought warmth and a measure of healing to my heart. After silently thanking God for each one of them, I thought, Yes, there is hope for me yet.

The laughter and fellowship helped to revive all of us. We decided to tackle Aaron's luggage.

While Uncle Rudd went to get the suitcase from the living room, I asked Aunt Nissa if they had finished going through the briefcase and if they'd found anything else of importance.

Waving a dismissive hand, she said, "Not much, just some rental forms and a calendar book for appointments."

Uncle Rudd hefted the suitcase up on Aunt Connie's kitchen table. Taking out his pocket knife, he said, "I've already checked. It's locked."

When the locks broke, Uncle Rudd turned it upside down and shook everything out onto the table. A thick, blue-colored envelope came out last and started sliding off the table. I caught it.

Holding it in one hand, I slipped the contents out of the opened end. I unfolded the papers and read the top line, "Oh my! It's Aaron Scott's Last Will and Testament!"

There was no sense in reading all the legalese out loud, so ignoring everyone's questions, I read it silently as fast as I could. It didn't take long, because it was pretty straightforward. Aaron Landon Scott, being of sound mind and body (at the time), had left everything he owned, including the marina, which included a townhouse on the premises, to Connie Rosalie Tanner. She was the sole beneficiary.

My first thought was "wow," but it was my second thought that gave me a sobering and chilling insight.

"Dixie dear, you're white as a sheet, is there something bad in that will?" Aunt Nissa asked.

"Uh, no, not really," I mumbled.

"Then tell us what it says, Dixie-gal."

Looking at Aunt Connie, I smiled. "Aaron Scott loved you so much that he left everything to you."

With trembling hands, Aunt Connie reached for the will and read it for herself. Uncle Rudd and Freedom moved behind her so they could read it over her shoulder.

Aunt Nissa kept her eyes focused on me, a puzzled look on her face. "I don't understand, dear, what made you look so frightened a minute ago."

The other three stopped reading, and Freedom frowned. "Yeah, I noticed the look on your face, too. What gives, Dixie?"

I desperately wished that my dark thoughts hadn't shown so clearly. But being confronted, I had little choice in the matter. I tried to choose my words carefully. "I was thinking, why did Aaron Scott make out a will and bring it with him? I hardly think it was meant as a romantic gesture. Surely he knew he was in danger. Why didn't he do something to protect himself? He never hid the fact that he was in town. All of that is strange enough, but it also brings up the thought that if the killer had succeeded in framing Aunt Connie for murder and the will was eventually found, a jury might convict her of premeditated murder. The will gives her a motive."

"Premeditated murder! Motive! I know what that means! It means they would fry my wrinkled old hide like a turkey in hot oil!" Aunt Connie dropped the will on the floor like it had suddenly turned into a live wire.

Throwing a protective arm around his sister, Uncle Rudd said, "It's a good thing we're here to protect you!"

"Yes, it is a good thing," I agreed. "Because with Aunt Connie out of the way, what incentive would anyone else have to catch this killer?"

"Well, if that killer thinks we would stop hunting him down like the polecat he is just because Connie got the chair, then he doesn't know we're blood kin to Tenacious Tanner!" Uncle Rudd proclaimed.

Ever pragmatic, Aunt Connie planted her hands on her hips. "Yes, but I'd still be dead, you old goat!"

"Now, everyone just hold on for a minute," Aunt Nissa interjected. "As it turned out, the killer didn't get a chance to frame Connie. We got to her before Otis could. Thank the Lord for His mercy. But I may be able to answer the question about why Aaron came back." Aunt Nissa held up a black leather appointment book. "Earlier when I looked through it, there wasn't anything that I could see I thought would help. But I think that's changed."

CHAPTER ELEVEN

Aunt Nissa started flipping through the pages of the appointment book. Coming to a stop, she said, "Here it is." Holding the book out toward us, she pointed. "See, Aaron has a doctor's appointment for ten o'clock in the morning."

She flipped a few more pages. "Two weeks later, there's another appointment with a Doctor Sweeney, and underneath, Aaron has written the word 'specialist.' From then on he has appointments with hospitals for a CT scan and some other tests, and he goes back to see this Doctor Sweeney a couple more times. He also has one more interesting appointment." Aunt Nissa flipped over a few more pages, held the book outward, and again pointed to a date. "See, he has an appointment with his lawyer. I think Aaron was very ill. Maybe dying. He came back to Kenna Springs because he had nothing to lose."

At first none of us said a word, we just stared at the words, "Lawyer, 3:00 p.m.," scrawled in black ink.

Almost whispering the words, Aunt Connie said, "You

mean Aaron figured if he was dying he no longer had a reason to stay away from Kenna Springs?"

Aunt Nissa nodded. "It makes sense, doesn't it?"

"It makes a lot of sense," Uncle Rudd said. "But we'd just be guessing at this point. I wish there was some way we could know for sure."

"Uh, I might be able to get some information," I volunteered. "I could call my secretary and ask her to look up this Doctor Sweeney and see what kind of specialist he is. That might tell us something."

The moment those words were out of my mouth, I remembered that I had never called Estelle back to find out what happened with poor Mr. Woodbine. That was not going to sit well with Estelle. But at this point, she wasn't going to be any madder tomorrow than she was already, and I was much too tired to deal with her tonight, so I hastily added, "I'll call her first thing in the morning."

"That's a dandy idea. But remember, you and Freedom are going over to Brogan's Ferry tomorrow to see what you can find out about Dolly from Chad Gunther." Uncle Rudd handed me a slip of paper. "I've got the address and directions written down for you."

Aunt Nissa put a gentle hand on Uncle Rudd's arm. "Speaking of tomorrow, it's going to be a big day for all of us. I think we'd better get on home."

Aunt Connie bent down and picked up the will. Carefully folding the pieces of paper, she sighed. "I don't want to deal with this right now. I guess I'll put it somewhere for safekeeping before I go to bed."

Before any of us could throw out a few suggestions on where that "safe" place should be, Aunt Connie walked over to her kitchenette, opened a cabinet, and retrieved a plastic food container. Grabbing a paper towel, she wrapped the will in it and carefully placed it in the plastic container. Snapping the lid shut, she put the container in the refrigerator.

Afraid that she might not know what she was doing, I asked, "The refrigerator? Why don't you put it in the safe you keep your deposits in overnight?"

Blushing slightly, Aunt Connie shrugged. "The refrigerator is the safe I keep my deposits in overnight. Who's gonna look in the refrigerator for valuables?"

She had a point. Aunt Connie has never kept much in the way of food in the refrigerator. Why not get as much use out of it as she could?

"I guess the fridge is about as safe as anywhere." Aunt Nissa reached for her now empty picnic basket. "Why don't Rudd and I get here early in the morning and cook breakfast for everyone?"

"There's no need for you to do that," Aunt Connie replied. "You've already been doing a lot of cooking. I have some of those toaster waffles in the freezer."

Before Aunt Nissa could comment, Freedom cleared his throat. "Tell you what. I make a mean biscuit and sausage gravy. How about everyone meet over at my place for breakfast, say about seven?"

Beaming first at Freedom then at me, matchmaking Aunt Nissa accepted on behalf of all of us, and it was settled.

After everyone left, Aunt Connie and I had a cup of hot tea together then took turns getting ready for bed in her elbow-room only bathroom.

Once in the guest bedroom, I cracked the window open a bit and crawled under the covers. As I lay there, I started going over the day's events in my mind. As I drifted off, I had the feeling that there was something I had forgotten.

Just before dawn I woke up slow and easy, forgetting for a moment where I was and why. Then it all came rushing back, including what I was trying to remember last night.

Aunt Connie was already up and making tea. Sitting down at the kitchen table, I asked, "Aunt Connie, do you remember that Latham told us that Truman Spencer was the one who told him that Aaron Scott was in town?"

"And good mornin' to you, too," Aunt Connie mumbled. "You want some tea? I need some time to get my peepers open before you tell me anything real important."

Deciding my observation could wait, I mumbled, "Yes, I would love some tea."

For the next several minutes we sipped our tea in companionable silence.

Finally Aunt Connie lifted her arms, stretched them outward, and softly groaned, "Getting old sure isn't the easiest thing a body has to do in this world. Nowadays, it takes me awhile to get to sleep. When I do, I don't sleep as sound as I used to. My back starts achin', and my hip starts hurtin', and by the time morning rolls around I'm stiff all over. Didn't used to be that way."

I didn't comment. I could see by the look on her face that there was a point to this conversation. She was gathering her thoughts, sorting them out. When she was ready she would tell me the rest.

"Last night, I. . ." Aunt Connie sighed and started again. "Last night I couldn't sleep. I kept thinking about all the stuff Aaron left me. I'm none too proud of it, I can tell you."

I reached out and put my hand over her hand. "There's nothing for you to be ashamed of, Aunt Connie. You should be touched. You should be amazed that Aaron left that will. He still loved you. Of course it would be on your mind."

Abruptly Aunt Connie got up from the table and poured herself another cup of steaming water. Grabbing a tea bag from the box on the counter, she stuck it in her cup and sat back down. "What I'm trying to tell you is that while I am touched and amazed, those weren't the only emotions, the only thoughts, whirling around in my feeble brain last night." She leaned forward. "I began to think about what I could do with all of Aaron's money. I even snuck out of bed last night and checked Aaron's bank account. I had myself spending that money on all sorts of stuff. Are you following me?"

I nodded, surprised not only at her thoughts, but her honesty.

"Good." Aunt Connie leaned back in her chair. "I just made myself sick of myself, if you know what I mean. So I had a little Sunday-go-to-meetin' talk with Jesus. I figured He would know what to do. After a while I knew what to do, too."

Leaning forward again, Aunt Connie's face beamed with excitement. "So, here's what I propose. Once the killer is caught and things settle down some, I would like to ask your folks to run the marina. They could live in Aaron's townhouse—rent-free, of course, and I would pay them a salary or a portion of the rent money from the slips. Now that takes care of the marina stuff. 'Course, that's saying your folks would agree to the arrangement, but I'm thinking they will. Last letter I got from 'em, seems like they were stretching themselves to make ends meet. What d'ya think so far?"

That must have been quite a talk with Jesus that Aunt Connie had. My heart flooded with gratitude at such a generous offer. I expressed those feelings to Aunt Connie as well as I could and told her that I thought they might go for running the marina.

"Good." Aunt Connie nodded. "Now I want to tell you the rest of my plan, and I want you to hear me out before you say anything. I'll give you your say after I'm through, so keep that mouth from flappin' ahead of time." Aunt Connie took a deep breath and then hit me with the surprise of my life. "Okay, here goes. I've worked hard all my life, and I got the aches and the pains to show for it. I think Peggy would like to buy me out, but she's not in any position to pay a fair-market price for this place. And up until last night I would have needed fair-market price just to live off of. That's changed now. I think I can offer Peggy a deal she and her husband can afford. I can retire. Oh, maybe help out now and again, just to keep my hand in things and keep life interesting."

"That's a great idea, Aunt Connie." I opened my flap.

Frowning at me, Aunt Connie held up a finger. "Hush, child. You already know that when your Grandma and Grandpa Tanner passed away, they owned quite a bit of farmland. That land mostly went to the boys because they were into cattle and farming, but I got the house and thirty acres on Willow Creek that they kept rented out. I never rented it, but I've kept it up over the years, figuring I would have to eventually sell this place and retire out there. But I like living in town, and I've never looked forward to living out at Willow Creek. As things stand, I can now buy me a little place right near the town square, or I can maybe work it out with Peggy just to stay right where I am. So, what I would like to do is to give you the house and thirty acres at Willow Creek." She gave me a stern look. "I know you'd like to start telling me why you can't accept my offer. I want you to remember, Dixie, I asked you to hear me out, so keep that flap shut, like I told you, till I'm finished."

I couldn't believe she was offering me Willow Creek. Although I had always admired, maybe even drooled over the craftsman-style house at Willow Creek, what would I do with it?

Smiling at me, Aunt Connie said, "I know what you're thinkin' 'bout now. You're thinkin' you can't accept my offer because you have a life in Little Rock. But I think you can have a life here, too, a real good life, Dixie. You don't have to quit being a psychologist, honey. There's plenty of insane folks in Kenna Springs. Half of 'em are probably kin to you. You could work out of the house. There's thirty acres out there, plenty of room for parking. And you'd own it, free and clear."

I felt myself tempted. But it just wasn't practical, was it? What about insurance and job security and all the other benefits that came with big-city life?

"I just don't know what to say," I told her. "I appreciate the offer, I do. A part of me would like to jump at the chance and say yes, but there are also a lot of no's rolling around in my head."

"Don't say no just yet, honey. Take your time thinking about it. There's no hurry. But do take it seriously. We'll keep this between ourselves for right now. When things are more settled we can talk about it again. Okay?"

I nodded meekly. Maybe Aunt Connie was right. Rather than just reject her offer, I should give it some thought. Coming back to Kenna Springs didn't sound like such a bad idea anymore.

"Mercy, child." Aunt Connie suddenly jumped up from her chair, grabbed both cups, and threw them into the sink like they were paper instead of ceramic. "Look at the time!

It's nearly seven o'clock. We've got to get dressed and get on over to Freedom's place."

That's Aunt Connie for you. Drop a bombshell at dawn's early light and then go eat breakfast.

Uncle Rudd and Aunt Nissa were coming up the stairs just as we walked out the door. We waited for them and walked to Freedom's place together.

Freedom already had the door standing open. We could see him by the stove, grinning and waving us in with a large spoon in his hand. "Hope you're hungry!"

"We sure are," Uncle Rudd answered for all of us. The four of us headed for the kitchen table and sat down.

Freedom took the biscuits out of the oven, ladled the sausage gravy into a large bowl, and set both on the table. Aunt Nissa served coffee; Uncle Rudd said grace and started passing the biscuits.

Aunt Nissa took a bite of her biscuit and raised her eyebrows in surprise. "Why, these are homemade biscuits, Freedom. Where did you learn to make homemade biscuits?"

"My dad passed away when I was a teenager, leaving mom to run our coffeehouse. To help out, my brother and I pretty much took care of things around the house, which included both of us learning how to cook."

"I'm so sorry you had to go through your teen years without your dad," Aunt Nissa said. "That must have been very hard on you and your brother."

"I'm sorry, too," Aunt Connie chimed in before Freedom

could answer. "But I gotta say these biscuits and sausage gravy rival yours, Nissa." To which Aunt Nissa agreed.

After that there was a void in the conversation until Aunt Connie said, "By the way, Dixie, what was it you were going to tell me this morning? Seems like it was something about what Latham said yesterday."

In all the hoopla of Aunt Connie's plans I had forgotten all about Latham. "Oh yes, when I asked Latham how he found out about Aaron coming to town, he said he thought it was Truman Spencer who told him. It just seems sort of strange that either Truman's name keeps coming up, or he keeps showing up himself."

"You still thinking Truman's our killer?" Uncle Rudd asked.

"Maybe." I shrugged my shoulders. "Anybody got anyone else in mind?"

Four shaking heads answered that question. Aunt Nissa finally broke the woeful silence with her usual brisk common sense.

"Then the best thing we can do for Connie right now is to concentrate on the things we can do. Dixie dear, have you called your secretary and asked her to check on that Doctor Sweeney?"

I felt the blood rush to my face. I had forgotten about calling Estelle because the easiest way to deal with Estelle is not to deal with Estelle. But I had to face the music, pay the piper, take my medicine. . . . It was decided that I was relieved from breakfast cleanup duty so that I could phone Estelle.

CHAPTER TWELVE

I let myself into Aunt Connie's apartment, found my purse, and dug out my cell phone. It was a little before eight in the morning. I decided to call the clinic number. Estelle usually comes in early.

She picked it up on the first ring. I heard her efficient office voice say, "Dr. Tanner's office, can I help you?"

"Uh, hi, Estelle, sorry I didn't call back yesterday, some, uh, things came up." I stammered, rubbing my stomach like that would somehow loosen the hard knot I felt forming inside it.

"How did things turn out with Mr. Woodbine?" I asked quickly. I didn't want to give Estelle a chance to ask me any questions about what I was doing in Kenna Springs. I had simply told her there were some problems with my family. I hadn't elaborated that those problems entailed murder and mayhem. I didn't particularly want to start elaborating now.

"The candy did not work." Estelle's voice was more than a tad frosty. That didn't bode well.

"How did Dr. Gaitherman coax him out of the coat closet then?"

"Dr. Gaitherman did not coax Mr. Woodbine out of your closet."

"I see." I felt the pace of my heartbeat pick up. "Estelle, are you telling me that Mr. Woodbine is still in my closet?"

"No, he is not in the closet," Estelle said. My heart, at least, went back to normal. She did throw me a bit more information. "Presumably he is at home, or doing whatever it is he does at this time in the morning."

I asked the next logical question, "Then how did he get out of the closet?"

"I. . .well. . .I got him to come out of the closet."

I couldn't believe what I was hearing. Estelle Biggs, who had never interfered in any of my counseling sessions, took it upon herself to extract a patient from my closet. This I had to hear.

"How did you manage to do that?"

"I went to the closet and informed him that if he continued to stay in that closet, I would be forced to bill him for 'closet time,' which, as it just so happens, is about twice your normal fee. He came out immediately. Before he left, he made an appointment to see you next week at his regular time."

Good for Estelle. Not the strategy I would have used, but it had obviously worked. Trying not to giggle, I moved on to the real reason for my call.

"Estelle, I hate to do this, especially after what you've been through, but I called for another reason besides checking on how things went with Mr. Woodbine. I know this isn't in your job description, but could you do me a favor and look up a Dr. Sweeney? He's a specialist, practicing in the Fort Walton Beach area of Florida. I need to know his specialty, his credentials, and his phone number."

When Estelle said, "Of course I can do that, Dr. Tanner," I knew we were back on solid ground with each other.

"Do you have any more information than that?" she asked. "Do you know his first name? It would make things easier if I knew a little more."

"I know it would, Estelle, but that's all the information I have. It's just a hunch, but you might try starting with oncology doctors."

I knew what Estelle really wanted to know was why I wanted information on Dr. Sweeney. That I could not tell her.

Making one more stab at getting something out of me, she asked, "Would you like me to make an appointment with Dr. Sweeney? Is it for your mom or dad? Don't they live in that area of Florida? Is someone in your family seriously ill, Dr. Tanner?"

I continued to hedge. "I know I'm being evasive about all of this, and that isn't fair to you. I really can't tell you what's going on. But I can assure you that no one in my immediate family needs to see Dr. Sweeney."

I heard her sigh. "All right, Dr. Tanner. I think I understand. Do you want me to call you on your cell phone when I find this Dr. Sweeney?"

"Yes, I'll leave my cell phone on and keep it handy." I was relieved. "And Estelle, thanks for understanding. Good-bye."

I had just put my cell phone back in my purse and started for the door when Aunt Connie walked in.

"You were gone so long we were gettin' kinda worried. Everything all right? Did you talk to your secretary? What's her name, Estelle?"

The thought went through my head that Aunt Connie could remember things like the name of a woman she had never met, and she had certainly been a tower of strength and encouragement when it counted. I wondered if maybe Uncle Rudd and Aunt Nissa had it wrong about her. Other than her reaction to Aaron's murder, which was understandable, she sure seemed to be in control of all her faculties. Maybe Aunt Connie forgot a few things before the murder because the stress of running her own business had been getting to her. Maybe her decision to retire was the right one for her.

"Everything's fine. I just had to answer some questions Estelle had for me about a client. She's going to look up Dr. Sweeney for us and call me back with any information she finds."

Once Aunt Connie and I were back in Freedom's

apartment, Uncle Rudd wasted no time issuing our orders for the day. Aunt Connie and Aunt Nissa would take care of the flower shop, Uncle Rudd would go visit his buddies from the bachelor party list, and Freedom and I would go talk to Dolly O'Connell's one time boyfriend, Chad Gunther.

By nine o'clock we were all on our way to take care of our appointed tasks.

Freedom and I sped and bumped our way down the two-lane highway toward Brogan's Ferry. The town was only fifteen miles from Kenna Springs. It always seemed longer because of the crooked roads.

Rolling the window down halfway, I let the cool air hit my face. Black clouds were overhead, and the humid scent of rain was in the air. Soon it would be winter, and the days of snow and sleet would come, but not today. Today it would rain.

Up ahead I could see the concrete slab bridge that crossed Twelve Mile Creek. Addison's Mill was just past the bridge. I remembered that Dolly's car was found not far from the mill, the halfway mark between Kenna Springs and Brogan's Ferry. I felt certain that Dolly had been murdered, but no one had ever found her body. Out loud, I posed the question, "If somebody did kill Dolly, where do you think they would have hidden the body?"

"I've been wondering that myself," Freedom said. "Seems like whoever killed her would have plenty of choices between the creek, the woods, and the mill. I guess since no one seemed to think she was murdered, no one went looking for her body when she was missing. The chances of finding her body now are about nil."

We had the directions to Chad Gunther's place of business that Uncle Rudd had given to me earlier. His auto repair shop was just outside the city limits of Brogan's Ferry. The faded sign on the top of a forlorn-looking concrete building told us we were at the right place. I noticed there was an older brown trailer in the back of the shop with a large black dog chained to the porch rail. Freedom parked the truck, and we walked toward the door with the word OFFICE painted on it. Freedom and I looked at each other and opened the door.

A long-legged man sat with his feet propped up on the metal desk in the middle of the room. A hank of thick, greasy hair hung down his forehead, almost covering one of his sullen eyes. Deep creases in his skin worked their way along his mouth and cheeks.

Moving his legs off the desk, the man's eyes fixed on me. Taking a long, leering, up-and-down look, he said in a gravelly voice, "What can I do ya for?"

"We're looking for a Mr. Chad Gunther." I put as much frost into the question as I possibly could, hoping this man was not Chad Gunther.

The man rolled his chair back and stood up. "Well, now, that'd be me."

He moved close enough to me that I could smell his stale breath. "I don't recall your name, girly. Did we meet down at

Jessup's Fishin' Hole Bar last Saturday night?"

Gunther put one hand on his chest, held the other up in the air, and danced a few steps with an imaginary partner. "Ho boy, I had one too many that night. I bet we had us a good time though, didn't we, girly?"

Out the corner of my eye, I noted that Freedom's face showed the same disgust I felt. I saw him move a step forward, but I held my hand out to stop him and shook my head. In the same frosty voice I had used a moment ago, I said, "Mr. Gunther, I assure you that we did not meet last Saturday night or any other Saturday night. If we had, you would have a distinct and specific memory of it."

"Why's that, girly?"

"Because if we had, you would've most certainly had to pay your dentist extra for fixing your teeth on Sunday."

His body stiffened, and he said in an exaggerated whining tone, "Well, excuse me! I had no idea the Ice Queen had come to pay me a visit."

While I didn't like the idea of being leered at, called 'girly,' or even 'Ice Queen,' it occurred to me that I didn't want to alienate him entirely. Besides, I didn't want a repeat of yesterday with Fog Whitman, so I started over.

"Look, my name is Dixie Tanner." I pointed to Freedom. "This is Freedom Crane. We came here to ask you a few questions, that's all."

Gunther looked at Freedom like he had just noticed him for the first time.

"Yeah, whatever you two want, make it fast, I got work to do." Gunther stared at us through sullen eyes.

This was getting more awkward by the minute. "Mr. Gunther, we've gotten off on the wrong foot here, and we don't want to do that. We need your help, and in return, we might be able to help you in a way. Forty years ago my aunt was to be married. The night before the wedding, there was a bachelor party for her fiancé, and then he disappeared. That same night your girlfriend, Dolly O'Connell, went missing. We think there might be a connection."

I hesitated for a moment, because I saw Gunther's face darken, and his eyes narrow to fleshy little slits. Not knowing why or what else to do, I went on talking. "I know that must have been a hard time for you. We wouldn't willingly bring up old wounds, but you've got to believe me, it's necessary that we do so. We may be able to find out what happened to Dolly that night as well as what happened to our friend. Please help us."

Red-faced with anger, Gunther took a couple of steps toward me. Freedom moved in between the two of us. I couldn't see Gunther, but I heard him yell, "What're you sayin'—that my Dolly and your friend ran away together? That's a filthy lie! You ain't gettin' nothin' outta me. You hear me! Get outta my place! Now!"

Neither Freedom nor I moved. I think we were too stunned.

I was looking at the back of Freedom's head, but I heard

him say, "Listen, buddy, you got it all wrong."

Then all of a sudden I wasn't looking at the back of Freedom's head anymore. I was looking at a fist coming straight for my face.

I can't say that I saw stars, exactly, but I did notice little lights going off inside my head. There was a moment of unbelief, then the pain.

I lay there, my back against the soft drink machine. I was aware of scuffling noises and loud words, but the sharp pain just below my eye took up the better part of my attention.

When my eyeballs synchronized again, I saw that Freedom had Gunther down on the desk. I couldn't quite catch what Freedom was saying to the man, but every once in a while he would bump Gunther's head on the desk for emphasis.

My head was spinning, but I forced myself to listen. In a voice that sounded far away, I heard Freedom saying, "All we want is for you to be nice enough to give us some information. That's the easy way to do things. The hard way is for me to keep thumping your head until you get some manners. Just let me know which of those two ways appeals to your sensibilities."

Gunther croaked out the words, "Okay! That first one's fine with me, man."

Freedom let him off the desk, but not off the hook. "Good choice. Stay put."

Freedom walked over to me and helped me stand up.

"What happened?" The words came out like I had a

mouthful of peanut butter. I held the left side of my face with my hand.

Looking somewhat sheepish, Freedom admitted, "Sorry. I ducked."

"You ducked?" Then the words came full circle inside my mind. "You ducked!"

"It was a reaction. I forgot you were standing behind me." Freedom gently took my hand away from my face. "Whew, that's going to swell up and be real ugly looking."

"Thank you for that diagnosis, Dr. Freedom," I snapped, putting my hand back on my face. I wondered just how long I would have to leave my hand there before my face went from real ugly to only sort-of ugly.

Freedom turned to Gunther and asked, "You got any ice?"

Gunther pointed toward a door. "In the garage. Ice is in the freezer."

"Anything to put the ice in?"

"Yeah, clean towels, third drawer down, next to the refrigerator."

Freedom fixed me a makeshift ice pack, and I held it on my face.

"You okay, Dixie? Gunther's ready to talk. He understands the situation now." Freedom turned to Gunther adding, "Don't you?"

Gunther nodded. The man looked like he'd spill his life story from birth on if we asked.

I grabbed the desk chair Gunther had been sitting in

when we came in, rolled it well away from both men, and sat down. "Mr. Gunther, I realize this has been a painful experience for, uh, both of us. But if you will just tell us what you know about the night Dolly went missing, then we can get our business here over and done with."

"Yeah, okay," Gunther said, rubbing the back of his head. "Me and Dolly had a thing going on for more than a year. It was sort of off and on. She'd get mad or I'd get mad, then we'd make up." Gunther lifted the corners of his mouth in what passed for a leering smile. "In the good times we sure had us some fun. Things seemed like they was goin' pretty good for a while there, but she started actin' funny. Breakin' dates, not bein' home when she said she would be, things like that. I began to suspect she was seeing someone else. Late one afternoon I called to ask her out. She told me she had other plans. Big plans. Made me so mad. We had us one huge fight. She admitted she was seeing someone, but she never told me who. Just said he treated her like a lady, something she didn't think I knew how to do. She said this guy was gonna marry her. According to her, they were gonna go away and live some kind of fancy life. After she told me that, I went down to Jessup's, had a few too many, and me and some buddies went fishing. I waited a couple of days, then I went back to her place to see if she had cooled down and come to her senses yet. She wasn't there. I figured maybe she really did take off with this guy. Just to cause her some grief, I called the police and reported her missing. They looked for her for a day or two, then they figured out I just wanted to get back at her, and they quit searching. That's it, the whole story." Gunther shrugged then hung his head down and added, "She was a wild one all right, but she could turn a man's insides to jelly by just smilin' real pretty. Sometimes I still miss her." He looked at me, shamefaced. "Sorry. I just can't stand to think of her with another guy, even after all these years."

Although the relationship between the two was obviously not a healthy one, I could see that at one time Gunther had feelings for Dolly. I hastened to reassure him. "Mr. Gunther, our friend is not the one Dolly was seeing. Do you have any idea who this man was? Any wild guesses or hunches?"

"Naw." Gunther shook his head. "She only said that when he put a ring on her finger, it would surprise everyone in Brogan's Ferry and Kenna Springs."

"Do you think, then, that this guy she was seeing was from Kenna Springs?" Freedom asked.

"Don't know for sure." Gunther shrugged. "Always thought so, though. There was talk around town that she was sneakin' around with some guy from Kenna Springs."

"What makes you so sure Dolly just ran off?" I prodded. "Couldn't something bad have happened to her? They found her car parked near Addison's Mill. Didn't that make you suspicious at all?"

Gunther sat down on the edge of the desk. "Naw, you have to know Dolly. She used to do all kinds of crazy stuff. She'd take off every now and again when she felt like it. When she came back, she'd tell me how sorry she was, and I'd take her back." Gunther went quiet, tracing an imaginary pattern in the dust of his desk with one of his fingers. "For a long time I thought she'd come back. She never did."

Just then I came the closest I would probably ever come to liking Chad Gunther. He loved Dolly and missed her. Everyone should have someone who missed them.

I rolled my chair a little closer and gently asked him, "So, you think she is still alive?"

Gunther's eyes widened, and I saw that he was on the verge of tears. "Sure I do. I always have." He stood up and turned his back to us. "And if she's not, I don't wanna know about it."

I looked over at Freedom and motioned with a nod of my head toward the door to let him know it was time to leave.

Freedom extended his hand to Gunther. "Sorry about the head thumping."

Gunther looked at Freedom's extended hand for a moment then reached out and shook it.

I handed Gunther what was now a sopping wet towel with melting ice in it, and Freedom and I left.

As we walked out the door, I heard the rumble of thunder. The rain would come soon. Maybe it was just the throbbing sensation from the swelling around my eye, but when I looked at the dark clouds, I felt a sense of foreboding.

CHAPTER THIRTEEN

The numbing effect of the ice pack was wearing off. Pain was taking center stage in my mind again by the time I got into Freedom's truck.

I put on my seat belt and frowned at Freedom. "You *ducked*!"

"I said I was sorry, and I really am." Freedom sounded sorry, but he was also grinning from ear to ear. "I suppose now I'll have to listen to you moan and groan all the way home."

"At the very least," I snapped.

Freedom backed the truck out then put his foot on the brake and stopped. Leaning over, he pulled a small plastic cylinder out of the glove compartment. Flashing a smile my way, he commented, "Maybe not," and took out two yellow earplugs and stuffed them in his ears. "I wear these when I'm working with my chainsaw." Then the man actually had the nerve to chuckle as we drove off.

All the way out of town I tried to figure out how to remove those yellow earplugs from his ears—accompanied by as much pain as possible.

I was still working out the details as we passed the city limits of Brogan's Ferry. A few miles later I glanced at the rearview mirror on my side and noticed a hay truck with a full load of hay turning from a side road and coming up behind us. Another glance told me that the hay truck was moving fast and edging up pretty close to the back end of the truck.

Tapping Freedom on the arm, I said, "You'd better let that hay truck pass us."

"What?" Freedom yelled.

"THE HAY TRUCK, LET IT PASS," I yelled back, pointing at the truck behind us.

Freedom looked in his rearview mirror and nodded. No one was coming from the opposite direction, so he moved his truck over to the shoulder as far as he could. Rolling down his window, he stuck his arm out and motioned for the hay truck to pass.

I was watching from the rearview mirror on my side as the driver looked like he was starting to pass then suddenly swerved into the bed of Freedom's truck.

Our truck started fishtailing across the road. All I could do was hang on to the door with one hand and the dashboard with the other and hope the seat belt held until Freedom could get the truck under control.

When he did, the driver in the hay truck hit us again. This time hard enough for Freedom's truck to spin in and out of a shallow ditch. I bounced high enough to hit my head. Freedom pressed down on the gas pedal and tried to outrun the hay truck.

I held on to the dash and yelled, "Whoever is in that hay truck wants us dead!"

"What?" Freedom yelled back.

"TAKE THOSE STUPID EARPLUGS OUT OF YOUR EARS," I yelled, pointing to his ears.

"Oh, yeah." He plucked them out and tossed them to me. The hay truck was edging up again. It didn't seem to be the time to worry about being neat and tidy, so I dropped them on the floor and braced myself.

"Can you outrun him?"

"I don't know, this is an old truck," Freedom answered, then he looked at the gauges on his dashboard and added, "Uh-oh!"

" 'Uh-oh'? What does 'uh-oh' mean?"

"It means I'm on empty. But I've usually got a couple of gallons left when it says empty. Don't worry, we'll make it."

"What about the bridge by Addison's Mill?" I asked. "If we can't lose this maniac by the time we get to the bridge, we're in trouble. One good bump on that flat concrete bridge, and there's nothing to stop this truck from diving right into Twelve Mile Creek. We'll be swimming home, providing we're still alive. If you have any ideas, now is the time to say so."

"Well. . .I have one idea," he said. "In the truck bed there's several glass jars of wood stain. They're packed in a cardboard box. One of us could climb through the back window, grab those jars, and throw them at his windshield. If he can't see where he's going, maybe he'll have a harder time hitting us." Then he added, "Of course, one of us is busy driving."

"Won't that make him madder?"

"You got any better ideas? The bridge is coming up."

At the moment there didn't seem to be any other alternative. I unbuckled my seat belt, turned around, and slid the back window open. I had started to climb out the window when another problem occurred to me. "What if he has a gun? Won't he shoot me?"

"If he had a gun with him, he would've used it by now to shoot out my tires," Freedom answered, keeping an eye on the hay truck. "Dixie, you'd better get through that window pretty quick. He's starting to close the gap."

Bad timing was the password for this nightmare. I no more than managed to get almost half my body out the window when I felt the rain starting to fall. I saw the flash of lightning and heard the *crack* of thunder overhead. I started wiggling my way out the window. Finally, my hands touched the truck bed. I made it! I was just at the point where I could ease my legs down, when the hay truck bumped us again. For a brief moment I was airborne, until gravity took over and I slid face-first across the wet metal truck bed. Every bone in my body vibrated, but I could move, no broken bones. I thanked God, sincerely, and crawled over to the box of clinking glass jars in the corner of the truck. I tried to drag the box over to the tailgate, but the rain made the cardboard soft and it tore. Praying it would be enough, I grabbed three jars and scooted backward to the end of the bed.

The rain started coming down harder, and I had to squint my eyes to see anything. I threw the first jar and heard the glass break on the pavement, but the hay truck kept coming. Freedom had told me to aim for the windshield. I threw the second jar. It hit the hood of the hay truck, rolled off, and broke on the pavement. I was getting better.

The hay truck hit us again. Freedom's truck swerved all over the road. I couldn't hold on to brace myself and was thrown from one side of the truck bed to the other before Freedom got the truck under control. I had the one jar left in my hand. Popping my head over the rim, I threw the jar as hard as I could.

It hit the mark and crashed dead center on the windshield of the hay truck. Still squinting in the rain, I saw the truck swerve from side to side and heard the tires squealing as the driver fought for control. But the truck was too heavy and the road too slick. It spun off the road, sideswiped a tree, and came to a lopsided stop.

I continued my squinty-eyed watch from the bed of Freedom's truck as the hay truck became smaller and smaller. At first I wondered why Freedom hadn't stopped to let me back into the cab, then I realized he wanted to put some distance between us and the guy who wanted to kill us. That was fine with me.

Freedom crossed the bridge and stopped the truck so I could get back in the cab. Dripping wet and shivering, I announced, "I don't think I'll ever be warm again."

"I turned the heater up full-blast, but it'll take a few minutes for it to kick in. You did real good, Dixie. We'd probably be dead by now if it weren't for you." Freedom took off his jacket, put it around my shoulders, and held me close, rubbing my arms and shoulders to give me more warmth.

Thanking him through chattering teeth, I laid my head on his shoulder and closed my eyes. I wanted to cry. I wanted to sleep. I wanted an ambulance. I wanted to laugh hysterically. I didn't know what I wanted. Except that I wanted to be warm again.

Finally I stopped shivering, and I knew what I wanted to do. Pulling away from Freedom and handing him back his jacket, I said calmly, "I think we should go back and see who the driver of that hay truck is. He's probably hurt or may even be dead. I don't think we have anything to fear from him, so it's safe for us to go back there. Whoever is in that truck is probably the same person who murdered Dolly and Aaron. And I want him turned over to the police. We can put an end to this today, right here, right now."

My body was hurting, I was wet and I was cold, but mostly I was angry and getting angrier by the minute. Angry that someone had so little regard for life that he would murder others, angry that all of us were now targets, angry that this murderer wanted us dead. As far as I could see, we could put an end to this man's madness by going back to that truck.

"Dixie, what if we drive back there to the hay truck and find out he isn't hurt or dead? Wouldn't we be giving him another chance at us?" Freedom asked.

"Okay, you have a good point. So, we won't drive. We can walk back there. If we stick to the woods, he won't see us, and we could get close enough to at least see who he is."

"Well, that might work," Freedom conceded. After opening the door on his side of the truck, he looked at me. "Wait here, and if I'm not back in thirty minutes, call Rudd on your cell phone and get out of here. You've got your cell phone with you, don't you?"

I said yes and grabbed the phone out of my purse. Putting the cell phone in my jacket pocket instead of back into my purse, I quickly opened the door on my side and hopped out. "Oh no, you don't. I'm going with you. And before you start telling me all the reasons I can't go, let me point out that I can't get any wetter than I already am, and this was my bright idea to begin with. If it makes you feel any better, this time I'll be the one to duck if it comes down to a fight."

Freedom threw up his hands in surrender, and we started off for the woods to make our way back to the hay truck.

Even though the rain had let up some, we still had to squint to see until we got into the woods. The trees not only provided some shelter from the rain, they made it easier for us to see where we were going. Neither of us spoke. We concentrated on getting through the woods as quickly and as quietly as we could, looking over our shoulders at any menacing sound.

When we saw the truck up ahead, we crouched low and eased toward it. We were at the edge of the tree line, just a few yards from the hay truck, when my cell phone started ringing. It was so unexpected that for a moment I couldn't think what was making that kind of noise. Pointing to my jacket, Freedom mouthed the word, "phone." I reached into my pocket and grabbed the cell phone. Flipping it open, I whispered, "Hello?"

Estelle whispered back, "Hello, Dr. Tanner. Why are we whispering?"

"Oh, uh, no reason, really," I said, trying to talk quietly, but not whisper. I turned my back to the hay truck and walked a few feet back into the woods. "Did you find out anything about Sweeney?"

"Yes, Dr. Sweeney is an oncologist. A very good one, from what I can find out. Dr. Tanner, are you all right?"

"I'm okay, Estelle. Thanks for the information. I have to go now." I started to press the END button, but I heard Estelle almost yelling, "Wait, wait, Dr. Tanner, don't hang up."

"I'm still here, Estelle, what's up?"

"Don't you want Dr. Sweeney's address and phone number? I even have his home number." Estelle's voice had a frantic edge to it. I hated not being able to tell her what was going on, but now was not the time to have a heart-to-heart talk.

"I really appreciate that, Estelle, but I don't need that information right now. Keep it handy, though, I may need those numbers later. Gotta go, Estelle. Goodbye." This time I pressed the END button. I owed Estelle a nice, expensive steak dinner, along with a well-edited explanation. Right now, there were other things going on. I powered off my cell phone so that I couldn't get any more calls and went back to where Freedom was standing at the edge of the tree line.

In a low voice Freedom asked, "I take it that was your secretary and you got some information on Dr. Sweeney?"

I told him that Dr. Sweeney was a highly respected oncologist. And if Aaron Scott went to see Sweeney and then his lawyer, more than likely he had risked coming back to Kenna Springs because he knew he was dying.

Frowning, Freedom picked up a small rock and threw it back into the woods. "That makes all this even worse! Aaron just wanted to spend whatever time he had left with Connie. Right now I'd really like the opportunity to stomp the guy that murdered him. I'd like to wring his evil little neck."

Freedom picked up another rock and threw it as hard as he could then took a deep breath and let it out. After a moment he ducked his head slightly. "Sorry. Got a little carried away."

I put my arm through his. Seeing his anger helped me put my own anger and frustration in a better perspective. "I know how you feel, Freedom. I've had those feelings also, but we need to figure out who killed Aaron and then let the law take its course. Getting even isn't up to us. We've already gone too far taking the law into our own hands as it is. All this makes me feel like we're between that age-old rock and a hard place."

Taking another deep breath, Freedom said, "You're right. I know you are." He put his hand over the one I had through his arm then nodded his head toward the hay truck. "Guess we'd better put our frustration aside and get back to the problem we have staring us in the face. While you were on your cell phone, I snuck a little closer. No one's inside, Dixie. Whoever was driving that truck must not have been hurt too badly, since he was able to take off before we got here. It'd be impossible to catch him by foot, and by the time we got back to the truck, he'd be long gone."

Freedom and I walked up to the truck in the misting rain. It looked like there was a pretty good dent on the driver's side where it was butted up against a tree, but the passenger door was wide open. No one was inside.

To say I was disappointed did not adequately describe how I felt at that moment. I stood there shivering from the wet and cold. My muscles were aching from being thrown around in the bed of Freedom's truck. The area just below my eye throbbed, and for the first time I noticed a stinging feeling on my cheekbone—probably a scrape or bruise from landing on my face. But somehow all of that seemed like the least of my problems. I had counted on the murderer still being in that hay truck, counted on this whole thing being over and done with. I expressed how I felt in the only way I knew how. I cried.

Freedom held me for as long as it took for me to stop crying. When I calmed down, he suggested that we take a look inside the truck, just in case whoever was driving it left something behind that would identify him.

That idea improved my attitude a notch and left me with some hope. I went to the passenger side and started rummaging through the glove compartment.

Pulling out the truck registration, I motioned for Freedom to come closer. "Look! The truck is registered to a Micah Bass. I know him. He and Uncle Rudd are good buddies. Micah owns a fairly good-sized farm outside Brogan's Ferry. It's a sure bet that Micah wasn't driving this truck, so whoever was driving it must have stolen it. Which doesn't help us a bit."

While Freedom was looking at the registration paper, an idea began to form in my mind. I thought I saw a way to salvage this mess. "You know, Freedom, that means that whoever stole the truck has to go back to Micah's property to get his own car. If we go back to your truck and head back to Brogan's Ferry, maybe we could pass him and recognize who it is. What do you think?"

Freedom shook his head. "I think it would be a real good idea, except that I'm about out of gas. I don't even know if I have enough to get us back to Kenna Springs, which is now closer than Brogan's Ferry. But even if I had the gas, what's to stop him from seeing us and trying to run us off the road all over again?"

Disappointed, I admitted that Freedom was right.

Knowing that Micah Bass would report the hay truck stolen, Freedom took a handkerchief out of his back pocket and insisted we wipe off anything we had touched. Then we headed on back to his truck.

The rain had stopped. All that was left was a cold breeze. I started shivering and chattering so much in my wet clothes that I thought there was a good possibility I wouldn't need to ride back to Kenna Springs in Freedom's truck, I could just shimmy my way home.

All the way to Kenna Springs, I watched the rearview mirror on my side, hoping to see a car I recognized. I didn't see any.

After Freedom parked in the alleyway, we got out of the truck wet, cold, and depressed, and made our way to the back door of the flower shop.

Aunt Nissa was in the workshop with an armload of red and white carnations when I walked through the door.

"Oh, mercy me, Dixie, what happened to your beautiful face?" Aunt Nissa dropped the flowers all over the floor, stepping on some of them as she made her way over to me. "Oh, honey, something awful must have happened. But don't you worry, you're with us now." Looking at Freedom, she said, "Are you all right?"

Before he could answer, I said, "Yeah, he's fine. He ducked."

"What?" Aunt Nissa said, looking confused.

Freedom grinned. "It's a long story, Nissa. Are Rudd and Connie around?"

Aunt Connie came into the workshop from the showroom. Slowly walking up to me, she took her time looking at the shiner that was forming around my eye. "Must have been a doozy of a fight! Did you win?"

"Connie Tanner! Dixie's hurt," Aunt Nissa said, shocked. "She needs sympathy right now." Then looking at my wet clothes, she added, "And a hot bath."

Aunt Nissa took charge. Turning to Aunt Connie, and in a no-back-talk-will-be-tolerated tone of voice, she ordered, "Close up shop, Connie. We don't need to deal with any customers right now." Without a word, Aunt Connie headed for the front of the shop.

She turned toward us and using the same tone of voice, ordered, "You two go on upstairs, get out of those wet clothes, and for goodness' sake take a hot shower and warm up. Rudd hasn't come back yet, but he'll be here soon. Then we'll talk things over."

Aunt Connie yelled from the front, "But I want to know now how Dixie got that shiner! I don't want to wait until Rudd gets back."

Aunt Nissa ignored her and concentrated on the task at hand. "Connie and I will be upstairs as soon as we can. Freedom, you come on over to Connie's apartment when you get changed and showered." Then giving each of us a gentle shove in the direction of the back door, she told us, "Go on now! Both of you get on upstairs."

We went.

Warmth hit me as I walked into Aunt Connie's apartment. It felt good. Once in the little bedroom, I quickly shed my wet clothes and wrapped myself in the old well-worn terrycloth robe I had brought with me. It felt like the best thing I'd ever had next to my skin. I took my clothes and put them in Aunt Connie's washer and headed for the shower.

The hot water loosened my tight, sore muscles. I stayed in the shower until the hot water ran out. Bundled up in my robe, I went back to the guest room and put on sweats and tennis shoes. While I was dressing, I could hear everyone gathering and talking together in the kitchen. They were getting ready for lunch. I closed my eyes and stood still for a minute, listening to dishes clanking, the refrigerator door opening and closing at intervals, and the sounds of their voices. They were good sounds, sounds of family and friends. I thought of past family reunions, Christmas and Thanksgiving gatherings. Sometimes life is good, and sometimes it is not. Considering we were risking our lives to catch a killer, this was one of those "not" times. Before I joined Freedom and my family in the kitchen, I couldn't help whispering a prayer of thanksgiving for each one of them.

"What's for lunch?" I asked as I joined the fray.

Aunt Nissa didn't waste any time hugging me. "Feel better, honey?"

"A little," I admitted.

Uncle Rudd, Aunt Connie, and even Freedom, who apparently showered faster than I did, either patted me tenderly on the back or hugged me. We might be a bunch of eccentrics, but we're a loving bunch of eccentrics.

"We're just having sandwiches and chips," Aunt Nissa said, taking my arm and leading me over to the kitchen table. Pulling out a chair, she motioned for me to sit down then grabbed a small package of frozen hamburger and handed it to me. "Here, I took this out of Connie's freezer for you. Hold this on your eye for a while, dear."

Obedient, but leery, I put the package to my eye. "Frozen hamburger? In the movies don't they use a piece of raw steak?"

Aunt Nissa shrugged apologetically. "It's all Connie had."

After Uncle Rudd asked the blessing, Aunt Nissa passed around the plate of ham-and-cheese sandwiches, followed by a bowl of chips. Aunt Connie poured iced tea into pink, blue, and green metal glasses and set them at each place, informing us that was all she had, like it or not.

Piling three sandwiches on his plate, Uncle Rudd said, "Freedom's been telling us what all happened this morning, Dixie-gal. I sure am sorry you two got into all that trouble."

"Me, too, but we're all in one piece and that's the important thing," I told him firmly, wanting to put Chad Gunther, followed by the ride of my life, far behind me. "What did you think about Doctor Sweeney turning out to be an oncologist?"

"Ah, I knew I forgot something when I was telling them what happened," Freedom said.

"If Sweeney is an oncologist, then Aaron was dying of cancer," Aunt Connie sighed.

"Sure looks like that might be the case, Little Sis." Uncle Rudd nodded.

Aunt Connie shoved her plate to one side. "I don't think I have much of an appetite right now."

"I don't blame you one bit," Aunt Nissa told her.

For a while there was an awkward silence at the table. We sat there, feeling terrible for Aunt Connie. Somebody needed to say something. Change the subject. So I did. "Did you find out anything today, Uncle Rudd?"

Uncle Rudd finished swallowing. "Not much, not much at all." He shook his head. "It's getting downright discouraging. I talked to most everyone, except Latham and Truman. None of the ones I talked to remembered much of anything, except for the fact that Aaron wouldn't set foot on Latham's boat."

My inner radar went to work. "You didn't talk to Truman? Where was he?"

"Don't know, Dixie-gal. I went by his office and his house. He wasn't at either place." Uncle Rudd cocked his head and gently shook his finger at me. "I know what you're athinkin'. Just remember, I didn't get ahold of Latham Sheffield, either."

Before I could answer, Aunt Connie suddenly plopped her glass of iced tea down hard on the table. "All Aaron wanted was to live out whatever days he had left. He was robbed of those days, and that makes me fightin' mad." Her whole body trembled with anger. "We got to do something to flush this murderin' buzzard out into the open. What's the old saying? Desperate times call for desperate measures. I say we're desperate. We need a plan!"

"I agree with Connie," Freedom said calmly. "So far we've turned over every stone we can think of and still don't know who the killer is. What we do know is that we are dealing with a man who thinks he can get away with murder. And in my opinion, he won't hesitate to murder any one of us." He cleared his throat. "And there's a couple more things we know about him now."

"What are they?" Aunt Connie gave him a puzzled frown.

"Number one, Aaron's killer is definitely responsible for Dolly's disappearance. If there were no connection between the two incidents, he wouldn't care what we could find out from Gunther, and so he wouldn't have tried to run us off the road after talking to him. And number two. . .he's watching us." Freedom's voice grew chill. "How else would he know where Dixie and I were? He must have followed us from Kenna Springs to Brogan's Ferry, seen us head into Gunther's shop, and hightailed it over to Micah Bass's to steal his hay truck so he could ambush us on our way home. None of us are safe until we expose him and hand him over to Otis."

That was a sobering thought.

Uncle Rudd was the first one to express out loud what we were all thinking. "Let's do it then! Anybody got any ideas how we might go about flushing this guy out in the open?"

Aunt Nissa, always practical, asked, "But don't we have to decide who we're going to flush out first? We can't try to flush out everybody that attended that bachelor party can we? We'll have to pick someone."

She was right. We couldn't tackle the whole bunch at once. We had to focus on one person at a time. I decided it was time to put in my two cents' worth. "It does make sense that we have to pick someone, and my vote goes to Truman Spencer as the one most likely to commit murder."

Freedom spoke up before anyone else. "Truman is the only one that's acted even a little suspicious. I agree with that. We know from Gunther that Dolly was seeing someone from town, and we know that it must have been someone at the bachelor party, but that doesn't tell us a lot, much less point the finger at Truman."

Everyone looked at me. I felt like a lawyer about to plead a weak case before a jury. "I realize we don't know for sure why Dolly was murdered. We've just now come to the point where we're pretty sure she was. Maybe Gunther is right, she did just run away and is probably on her third or fourth marriage by now. But we've assumed she was murdered, and because Aaron Scott knew she'd been murdered, it scared him so badly that he left town. And of course, we've assumed the same information that scared Aaron also got him killed when he came back. We're assuming a lot of things, but they're at least educated guesses. That's all we have to go on. We do know that Truman lied to Otis about being on his way to the office when the burglary happened. We also know that Truman saw at least the heading on the article about Dolly. And from Latham Sheffield we know that Truman was aware that Aaron was in town. Last, but certainly not least, we know Truman was one of two people who wasn't around town today. So, taking another educated guess, I think we have to put Truman at the top of the suspect list."

"There is a sort of twisted logic in that," Freedom said. "Bottom line, we have to focus on somebody, and at this point, maybe Truman is the best we have. Whatever plan we come up with, let's keep it simple. No frills. We've got enough to worry about as it is."

"All right." Uncle Rudd nodded and looked at each one of us. "If we're all agreed, then after lunch we'll decide on a simple, no-frills plan to flush out Truman Spencer."

We all agreed.

CHAPTER FOURTEEN

After lunch we settled down in Aunt Connie's living room. Aunt Connie, Aunt Nissa, and I took the couch. Uncle Rudd and Freedom took the two chairs facing the coffee table on either side of the couch. Each of us, fortified with a cup of coffee, settled in for the long haul.

It took nearly two hours, a dozen sheets of paper, a few arguments, and one snack break, but we had a plan. A simple, no-frills, two-step plan.

The first step would be to call Truman Spencer to tell him we would give him an interview about the burglary. We would invite him over to the flower shop and tell him to use the back entrance. We decided, largely on my say-so, that placing him at the scene of the crime would have a psychological impact on him, making him more nervous and vulnerable. The second step would be to ask him some very leading and pointed questions about Aaron Scott and Dolly O'Connell. We hoped that steps one and two would cause Truman to become so nervous and frustrated that he would do something stupid. Then the five of us would pounce on him and turn him over to the sheriff.

It's just barely possible that our plan wasn't the most brilliant way to handle things. But it was the best we could come up with.

Uncle Rudd made the call from Aunt Connie's bedroom while we waited quietly in the living room.

"I got ahold of him at the newspaper office," Uncle Rudd said as he came out of the bedroom. "Ol' Truman said he had some stuff to take care of first, but he can be here at seven tonight. Sounded downright pleased to be coming over."

The fact that Truman had almost four hours before he came over made me uneasy. "Truman may be concocting his own little evil plan to do away with us. He certainly has the time for it. We had better be ready for him."

Uncle Rudd nodded, then turned to Freedom. "Let's you and me go downstairs to the workshop and take a look-see. We have as much time as Truman to figure out the best way to protect ourselves."

"I think Connie and I might be of some help," Aunt Nissa said. "We'll go downstairs with you." She patted my knee. "Dixie dear, you've already had quite a day. You must be sore and hurting all over. Why don't you take a nap for a couple of hours? We'll be sure to wake you up in plenty of time to get in on the action."

Get in on the action. I decided that Aunt Nissa had been reading way too many mystery novels. She was right about one thing, though, my body was sore and aching. A nap sounded wonderful, and I told her so as I stood up and grabbed the small of my back with both hands.

Sitting there on the couch for so long had stiffened my body considerably. Taking a few careful steps in the direction of the kitchen, I faced everyone. "You go on downstairs. Have all the fun you want to. I'm going to get a glass of water, take a couple of extra-strength aspirin, and try to sleep."

As I climbed into bed, it occurred to me that no matter how much planning they did between now and when Truman showed up, if Truman came in with guns a-blazin' there wouldn't be much we could do to protect ourselves. I was so tired, even that thought couldn't keep me awake.

It didn't seem like I had been asleep for more than five minutes before Aunt Connie came barreling into the bedroom. "Time to get up, sleepyhead! There's a cup of hot coffee for you on the kitchen table. Come on now."

Once Aunt Connie was satisfied that I was wide-awake and sitting at the kitchen table, she left me with a cup of coffee in my hands and went back downstairs.

I looked at the kitchen clock. It was six fifteen. Forty-five minutes before Truman would show up. I had time to sip my coffee slowly and enjoy it.

As I sipped, I looked around the kitchen and living room area and was struck, for maybe the first time, with the color Aunt Connie had woven into her small living space. The furniture was getting older and a little faded, but that didn't distract from the bold color scheme and rich shades of greens, plums, and wine. She also had a love for brightly colored handcrafted knickknacks, as well as antique furniture. It was a nice place. Cozy. Peaceful. Quiet.

I wholeheartedly wished I could just stay in this apartment instead of going down to the workshop. I wasn't anxious for any more "action," as Aunt Nissa put it. But the sooner we got this over with the better. I put my empty coffee cup in the sink. I did a few stretches to loosen up my stiff body, then I brushed my teeth and headed out the door.

It was already dark, and I was glad that Aunt Connie had thought to flip on the porch light over her apartment as well as the bright light in the alleyway just outside the workshop door.

My first thought when I opened the door and stepped into the workshop was that they had been very busy little worker bees while I was asleep.

"What do you think about what we've done to the place, Dixie?" Aunt Connie asked, grinning from ear to ear.

I didn't know what to think. The place looked like a Halloween nightmare. They had hung fake cobwebs in all the corners of the workshop, put black crepe paper over the workshop table, and strewn dried or dead flowers all over the floor. On the work spaces butted next to the wall there were several half-dead, half-done flower arrangements. That was macabre enough. But the worst, and possibly most bizarre figment of someone's imagination, was the plastic skeleton laid out on the center worktable. The skeleton was sporting a blond shaggy wig, and its arms were folded across the chest, holding a bouquet of dead flowers.

Aunt Nissa and Aunt Connie stood next to me, both beaming at their handiwork. "Isn't it grand?" Aunt Nissa asked with a sweep of her arm. "We remembered what you said about bringing Truman back to the scene of the crime for the psychological impact. We think we added to that. Don't you?"

Yes, ma'am. I certainly thought they had added to the psychological impact all right. I know it made me uncomfortable.

Aunt Nissa looked disappointed. "Dixie dear, you don't seem to be very impressed. Do you think we went over the top just a bit?"

Deciding to make the best of it, I took a deep breath. "I think you accomplished what you set out to do."

They beamed at me again.

Uncle Rudd walked over to the three of us. "Okay ladies, it's our turn to tell Dixie our plan."

Frowning, Aunt Nissa put her hands on her hips and faced Uncle Rudd. "I just don't like it. I think we can do this without any guns."

Guns. The pit of my stomach tightened into a hard knot.

"It's only one handgun, Nissa," Uncle Rudd said defensively. "It's not like we have an arsenal of firearms."

Freedom joined us. "Look, I'm not crazy about waving a

gun around, but Rudd and I think we should be prepared. We've all agreed that whoever murdered Aaron and Dolly is dangerous. He's scared and thinks killing is his only option. If we're right and Truman's our man, then it doesn't make much sense for us to gather in one place where he can take potshots at us without being able to defend ourselves."

Folding his arms across his chest, Uncle Rudd nodded. "That's absolutely right. The gun stays."

"Well, it's too late to argue about it anyway," Aunt Connie said and pointed at the workshop clock. "Look at the time! We've only got a couple minutes before Truman arrives."

"Right. Places everybody," Uncle Rudd commanded, shooing everybody with his hands.

Freedom moved quickly over to stand near the workshop door and flattened himself against the wall so that he would be hidden when the door opened. He stood holding the gun in a ready position with both hands.

Aunt Connie and Aunt Nissa scurried over and stood on the other side of the center workbench, so that the workbench was between them and the back door.

"Remember, ladies, Freedom and I packed the space underneath the workbench, so if there's any shooting, you just duck and you'll be all right. Don't let Truman maneuver you away from that bench." Uncle Rudd grabbed what looked like a broom handle and walked over to the other side of the door from where Freedom stood.

Everybody was in place but me. "Where am I supposed

to be, Uncle Rudd?"

"Sorry, Dixie-gal. I forgot you weren't here when we decided these things. We've placed you in the corner workspace. You stand right by those two tall metal trash cans. Freedom has already filled them up with wood, so if any shootin' starts, you just curl up behind those cans and stay put."

I walked over and stood where I was told just as we heard a car pull up outside in the alleyway.

When we heard the knock on the workshop door, Aunt Connie yelled, "Come on in, Truman. It's not locked."

When the door opened, I saw Truman's eyes widen and his mouth drop open at the nightmare scene my aunts created. Then I heard a loud *pop*, the sound of glass crashing, and another loud *pop*. Truman fell forward into the workshop.

Uncle Rudd dragged Truman clear of the doorway. Freedom shot into the darkness outside until Uncle Rudd could slam the door shut and lock it. Aunt Connie screamed, and Aunt Nissa yelled for Uncle Rudd to be careful. I kept thinking this wasn't real. This couldn't be happening.

Uncle Rudd pointed at me. "Dixie-gal, get over there and turn off the lights. Connie, can you get to a flashlight?"

I was stunned and couldn't move until he yelled at me a second time and told me to get a move on. I felt this sudden surge of energy course through me, and I moved to turn off the lights. At the same time, Aunt Connie, with the flashlight already turned on, quickly made her way over to Uncle Rudd, who was kneeling beside Truman. Shining the light on Truman, she asked with a shaky voice, "Is he dead, Rudd?"

"No, but he's bleeding pretty bad. Somebody needs to call an ambulance."

Aunt Nissa had already started toward the wall phone. "I'll do that. I know the number." Then, pointing to a drawer, she told me to get some aprons out of it and use them for bandages. I opened the drawer and grabbed three or four.

I folded the aprons into squares, trying to keep my hands from shaking. "Can't we turn on the lights?"

"Nissa, close the workshop curtain," Uncle Rudd said. "Then we can turn the lights back on."

Relieved that I could see what I was doing, I knelt down next to Truman and bandaged him up the best I could. I applied as much pressure as I dared to stem the bleeding.

I felt tears forming in my eyes as I stared at Truman's still body. I prayed desperately for him to live. This was my fault. I had been so sure he was the murderer.

"The ambulance will be here any minute," Aunt Nissa said. Then kneeling beside me, she looked into my misery-filled eyes. "Dixie dear," she whispered, "I can do this. Let me help you."

I shook my head. "No, I have to do something."

Still looking at me with her soft brown eyes, she nodded. "Okay, darling, I understand. But you needn't think this is your fault. We all agreed, remember."

Yes, we all agreed, but only because I insisted. At the

moment I wasn't very proud of myself or my arrogance.

Interrupting my thoughts, Uncle Rudd said firmly, "He'll live, Dixie-gal."

At those words I felt my heart beat a little faster. "Are you sure?"

"I'm sure. The wound is too high up on the back of his shoulder to be fatal."

Knowing that Truman would be all right released me from my own tortured thoughts long enough for me to look around. "Where's Freedom?"

"After we turned out the lights, he went to the front of the shop," Uncle Rudd answered. "Odds are the killer left after Freedom shot back. But just in case he didn't, we figured he couldn't get through the window in the workshop, and this building is brick, so the only way the killer could get at us is if we opened that back door again, which we ain't gonna do, or by breaking the door or the windows in the front of the shop. So until the ambulance gets here, Freedom's keeping watch in front."

Sounded good to me, but what sounded even better was the ambulance siren getting louder and closer.

Freedom flipped on the lights in the front of the shop and pulled back the dividing curtain before he came back into the workshop. "Ambulance is pulling up outside. How's Truman?"

"He's bleeding pretty bad, but he'll make it," Uncle Rudd told him and stood up. "Connie, you'd better go ahead and unlock that front door."

Aunt Connie grabbed her keys and sprinted to the front. As soon as the EMTs were inside, she pointed them toward the workshop. The rest of us got out of the way so they would have room to work.

I was relieved to see the ambulance team. I wasn't relieved to see Otis and his deputy, Billy, coming in right behind them.

Otis ignored us and watched the EMTs put an IV in Truman and pack his shoulder. When they had him on the gurney, Otis asked, "Is he going to be okay?"

"Probably," the EMT said. "The doc can tell you more after we get him to the hospital."

Otis ordered Billy to follow the ambulance to the hospital, and if Truman regained consciousness to take his statement. Once they were out the door, Otis turned his attention toward us. He eyed each of us in turn, spending a full extra minute with his gaze leveled on the gun in Freedom's hand and another staring at my swollen face. "Somebody want to tell me how Truman ended up getting shot in the back?" His voice was low and calm.

None of us felt the need to speak right up and tell Otis anything.

Otis narrowed his eyes and took a deep breath. "Okay. . . Nissa, you made the call. Let's start with you."

Flustered, Aunt Nissa started picking at the ruffle on the collar of her dress. "Oh, well, Otis, it's—well, it's a very long story, you see."

Otis waited. When Aunt Nissa didn't elaborate on that very long story, Otis glanced around the room. "I got the time to listen." His voice sounded chilly. He reached over and picked up the left leg of the plastic skeleton on the center workbench. Looking at it oddly, he added, "I come over here, and not only do I find that Truman Spencer has been shot in the back, I find this place looking like some kind of freak show. So, I'm pretty certain things ain't quite right. Now, one of you had better talk to me pretty quick before I decide to lose my temper."

When no one else volunteered to say anything, I did. "Otis, you've got to believe us. All of this started because we just wanted to keep Aunt Connie out of jail."

Otis's eyebrows shot up "Jail! Why would Connie go to jail?"

"Because someone has been trying to frame my baby sister for murderin' Aaron Scott," Uncle Rudd bellowed. "And we don't aim to let her go to jail for somethin' she didn't do. That's why!"

At Uncle Rudd's revelation, Otis simply looked dumbfounded.

When Otis finally got hold of himself, he no longer looked like the cheerful, intelligent, easygoing man I had always been around. He looked more like a man in dire need of anger management training.

When he bent down and peered into Uncle Rudd's face, I was extremely glad that he wasn't speaking to me. "Murder,

Rudd? Did you say that Aaron Scott has been murdered? I thought he left town. Just how is it that you know Scott is dead?"

I could see that all the bellow had gone out of Uncle Rudd, at least for the moment. Aunt Nissa edged closer to Uncle Rudd and pulled at his shirt sleeve. When Uncle Rudd looked at her, she quietly said, "It's best that we let Otis in on everything. You and Freedom show him, Rudd."

"Yes, I think that would be best," Otis commented dryly.

Uncle Rudd nodded at Freedom, and they started moving toward the flower cooler. Otis followed them. Uncle Rudd opened the cooler door and pointed inside. "In here, Otis."

Neither Freedom nor Uncle Rudd made a move to go inside. They positioned themselves, one on each side of the door. Throwing them a puzzled look, Otis stepped inside the cooler.

First we heard the crinkling noise of the pink cellophane, then a spate of words that made Aunt Nissa gasp and Aunt Connie blush.

Otis stuck his head out of the cooler, looked around at all of us. "That's Aaron Scott you got on ice in this cooler!"

When I heard Aunt Connie mutter under her breath, "We knew that, ya big oaf!" I nudged her and whispered, "Now is not a good time to get sassy."

Otis went back into the cooler for a few minutes. Then he came out and shut the door. Laying his forehead against the cooler door, he muttered under his breath, "I gotta get outta this line of work. Been saying that for years, but I have to admit, this may do the trick."

He wasn't taking this as well as I had hoped he would. I could sympathize, though. Maybe, given time, Otis would warm up to the idea a little more. I had.

Otis rubbed his forehead, closed his eyes, took a deep breath, and opened his eyes. He faced us. "Okay, I see what's happening. No, no, that's not true at all. I don't. But. . .I will see. So, what we'll do is this. We'll take a little trip over to the station. We'll all sit down, and you people will tell me a lot of things. And, when you've told me everything. . . and I mean everything, I will decide what to do with you. Understand? You'd better grab your jackets. It's a mite chilly outside. We're going to be walking over to the station. Billy and I rode over together, and he has the squad car."

We got our jackets and followed Otis.

CHAPTER FIFTEEN

Once inside the station, Otis pointed to the coffeepot and a plate of Martha's homemade cookies and told us to help ourselves. We did. I don't think any of us had eaten supper, at least I hadn't.

Once we demolished the cookies, Otis took us into his Spartan-looking office. When we were seated, Otis sat on the edge of his desk. "Okay, one at time. Rudd, you first. Tell me exactly what's been going on."

By the time Otis finished extracting the whole sordid tale, the bold-faced clock on the wall behind his desk read nine forty-five.

Even with knowing that we were all probably facing not only this night, but maybe many nights in a jail cell, Aunt Connie could hardly keep her eyes open. It had been a long and bizarre four days. I didn't blame her one bit. I was beginning to think that a nice stiff cot might be welcome myself.

Otis wasn't going to make it easy. After he had asked all the questions he wanted to and we had spilled our guts, he quietly sat on the edge of his desk, picked up a pencil, and started turning it upside down, then right side up; eraser then lead point, eraser then lead point. It was almost hypnotic.

Uncle Rudd was the first to cave in. Clearing his throat, he said, "If you're going to throw anybody in jail, Otis, it ought to be me. I'm responsible for this mess."

Aunt Nissa patted Uncle Rudd on the leg and firmly said, "No, dear, if you go to jail, we'll all go to jail."

Otis threw the pencil down and stood up. Hitching his thumbs in his belt, he said, "Folks, you're so used to taking the law into your own hands that you've forgotten it's not up to you. It's up to me to decide just who I will or will not throw into the slammer."

Otis walked around our five chairs. "Now technically, I can put all of you away for a good long time. Let's see, there's obstructing justice, withholding evidence, aiding and abetting. Course, that's just the beginning. I'm sure there must be some kind of law against putting a poor departed soul on ice and carting him all over the countryside. Are all of you getting the picture here?"

I know I was. At this rate I could put off the decision whether to move back to Kenna Springs or stay in Little Rock indefinitely. I hoped my new roomy was a neat freak.

Otis walked around the chairs again, letting us stew in our imaginations. Then he sat down on the edge of his desk again.

"I have a question, Otis," Aunt Nissa said calmly.

"Yes?"

"Do you think you could possibly arrange to put Dixie, Connie, and me next to each other in jail? And if you could keep Rudd and Freedom together that would be nice also. You see, we're family. Well Freedom isn't related, but he's like family, and we won't know anyone in jail. . .so I just thought. . ."

Otis held up his hand for Aunt Nissa to be quiet. I thought I saw the corners of his mouth twitch, but he got up and turned away too quickly for me to be sure. He walked around his desk and pulled out his desk chair and sat down. Then he leaned back and looked like he was thinking things over.

"Nissa," he said, "I'm going to answer your question, if you'll bear with me here." Then leaning forward and crossing his arms on the desk, he took a long look at us. "You know that I was born and raised in Kenna Springs. I know the people in this town, am related to a good portion of them. On the whole, I'd say that the good people of Kenna Springs generally take care of their own. 'Course, for quite a few generations now, you Tanners have taken the notion of caring for your own to the point it has become an obsession, and it seems like you haven't changed your minds any about that. And I think it's safe to say that the people in this town generally have a sense of justice. We like to see the good guys win and the bad guys lose. 'Course, ever since old Tenacious rode into town with that dead horse thief and insisted they hang that thief anyway, you Tanners seem to take it real personal-like that you have to see to it that justice is done."

Otis leaned even farther across his desk and pointed his finger at us. "But I would like to go on record here as saying that your attitude toward family and justice is just not right. No, sir, it is not right at all. It's not balanced, you see, not balanced one little bit. And it's got you nothing but trouble. Are any of you hearing me on this?"

There were a lot of "yes, sir's," "uh-huh's," and "I hear you loud and clear's" coming out of all five of our mouths.

"Good!" Otis slapped his hand on top of the desk. "Now, given the general attitude of the townsfolk around here, I know that if I put you folks in jail, then I'll have to listen to a lot of folks complainin' that you only did what you had to do. They'll stop me on the street. They'll stop me in the stores. They'll even call my house to tell me that I oughta be puttin' the real criminals behind bars instead of folks like you, who are just tryin' to do the best they can. And you know what else they'll say?"

All of us indicated in one way or another that we hadn't a clue.

"They'll say that the Tanners have always been a bit batty, and I shouldn't put you away for being batty. Of course it won't occur to them that you broke the law, and I'd be upholding the law. Nope, that won't occur to them at all. So, I'm gonna save myself a whole lot of grief. I'm not going to charge you folks with one blessed thing."

Relief, amazement, gratitude, are just a few of the emotions I felt when I heard Otis say that he wasn't going to put us all in jail. And from the reactions of the others, I would say they were feeling much the same way. We hugged, slapped each other on the back, thanked Otis several times, slapped him on the back, and then went back to hugging each other. Otis let us carry on for a little while and get it all out of our systems, then he held up a restraining hand and announced, "Now, settle down. I ain't quite finished yet. There's some things we have to agree on."

All of us immediately sat back down and paid attention.

"Okay, first off, you got to put Aaron Scott's body someplace else besides that cooler, and you need to do it as soon as possible. No one but the six of us is to ever know that body was in Connie's flower cooler. I don't even want Billy to know anything about this. It just ain't a fittin' place for a body. But even if it were a fittin' place, that flower shop is now a crime scene. Billy will be going over every inch of that place, and if that body is found there, then the killer won't have to worry about where you folks stashed Aaron. For your own safety we need to keep him guessing. I don't want anyone else shot. So get Aaron out of there!"

All of us started speaking at once, giving our opinions about where to put Aaron's body, but Otis put his hand up again and commanded us to shut up.

"Don't be interruptin' me before I'm finished talkin' to you folks. I don't want to know where you put him until after

I find the killer. Understand? Now, another thing. Rudd, you get those shears from wherever you've stashed 'em and bring 'em to me first thing in the morning. If I can't have the body, I at least want the murder weapon."

Uncle Rudd couldn't bob his head fast enough.

"Okay, now I want to impress upon you folks the seriousness of what you've done. You've not only made yourselves accessories to murder, you've put me in an awkward position. I don't know what to say to the D.A. I could lose my job. Be arrested myself. I don't much like being put in that position. I don't know when or how I'm going to explain this to Billy, much less put it all down in an official report. And the worst of it is that because of your interference, Truman Spencer got shot tonight."

"Whatever you decide to do, Otis, every one of us will back you to the hilt," Uncle Rudd said firmly.

"Thank you, Rudd. Now shut up." Otis narrowed his eyes. "I'll manage. Your job is to stay out of this from here on out. If anyone asks you, just tell them that you weren't much help at all. And let me say that if you don't abide by these conditions, I'll slap every single one of you in jail faster than you can say 'vote for Otis for sheriff,' and hang the complaints from the townsfolk. Have I made myself very, very clear?"

Uncle Rudd stood up, and we followed suit. He reached out his hand to Otis and Otis took it. As they shook hands, Uncle Rudd told him, "Otis, I'm mighty grateful to you for not putting us in jail. We'll do as you say and take care of

Aaron's body as soon as possible. In fact, we'll take care of it tonight."

Aunt Connie stepped in front of Uncle Rudd. "Otis, would you mind calling the hospital and checking on Truman before we leave? We'd all like to know how he's getting along."

Otis nodded. "Okay, you go on out to the waiting room, and I'll be out there in a minute with whatever I can find out."

We were a pretty solemn lot as we filed out into the waiting room. We were talked out, tired, and relieved about not going to jail, but still worried about Truman. Fortunately, it didn't take long for Otis to come out and tell us that Truman was out of surgery and doing well.

I desperately wanted to go to the hospital and see for myself that he was going to be fine. But it was already late, and we still had to figure out where we were going to bury Aaron.

Giving me an understanding look, Aunt Connie asked Otis, "Would it be all right with you if we went over to the hospital tonight to see Truman for ourselves? That is, if everyone else agrees. I know it would help me a sight if I could just lay eyes on him. And I think it would help the others, also—especially Dixie. We're all tired, but I think we got just enough energy left in us to at least check on Truman before we take care of Aaron's body. That wouldn't be too much to ask, would it, Otis?"

A thoughtful look crossed Otis's face before he answered.

"Yeah, I'm okay with that. Just don't tell Truman anything about Scott if he regains consciousness while you're there, all right? You don't have to get Scott's body out of the flower shop tonight. However, he needs to be out of there by mid-morning. I won't be able to hold Billy off from checking your place much longer than that."

We assured Otis we would take care of things and said good night. Then we got our jackets on and headed back to the flower shop. Uncle Rudd's car was still parked in the alley. He could drive us to the hospital from there.

The air was cool and crisp. The night sky was clear, and the stars shone as I looked up at them. I was glad to be walking out of the station a free woman, glad that Otis knew about Aaron Scott, and very glad that Truman Spencer was going to be all right.

I had just about talked myself into believing that we had come out of this safe and sound, and everything would turn out all right, when Aunt Connie pointed out that if the killer was watching us walk back to the shop, he could pick us off like crows on a fence.

We picked up our pace, with Uncle Rudd and Freedom walking on the outside, and tried to stay in the shadows all the way back to the flower shop. Once inside, we locked the doors, turned on the lights, and breathed a little easier.

Aunt Connie looked around the workshop and visibly shivered. "I'm sort of sorry now that we made this place look so spooky. But I sure don't have the inclination or the energy at the moment to clean it all up."

Uncle Rudd put his arm around Aunt Connie. "It's been quite a night, all right. We're all tired and worn out and still got a lot to do. We need to take care of Aaron's body, and we all want to check on Truman. So how about we take care of those two things at once. It came to me that Addison's Mill might be a good place to bury Aaron, at least temporarily. That old mill is abandoned, and nobody goes poking around out there. You ladies can take the car and go on out to the hospital to see Truman. Freedom and I will take his truck and Aaron's body and follow you. But we'll stop at Addison's Mill and bury Aaron. After this morning's rain the ground will be soft enough to dig a shallow grave. After we're through, we'll follow you ladies on to the hospital and meet up with you there. How does that sound to everyone?"

Aunt Connie sighed and nodded. "That's all right with me, Rudd. I think I would rather go on to the hospital. I don't know that I could bear seeing Aaron put in a shallow grave, anyway. Somehow that seems worse than putting him in the flower cooler. I'd like to see him have a proper burial, not just a shallow hole in the ground."

Uncle Rudd looked tenderly at Aunt Connie. "Once Otis gets this thing straightened out, we'll give Aaron a proper burial."

"Yes, I think it's best for everyone that you and Freedom bury Aaron," Aunt Nissa said to Uncle Rudd. "But after we see Truman, I don't think that Connie, Dixie, and Freedom ought to come back here tonight. It gives me the willies to think that the murderer could come back here. They should pack an overnight bag and come on out to our place and spend the night."

"When you're right, you're right," Uncle Rudd told Aunt Nissa. Then he turned his attention to the rest of us. "What d'ya say? Sound like a plan?"

The thought of spending the night in Aunt Connie's apartment over the flower shop, even with Freedom just next door, gave me the willies, too. I liked the idea of spending the night out at Uncle Rudd and Aunt Nissa's place and said so. Aunt Connie wasn't overly anxious to stay at her apartment either. It took a little while for us to convince Freedom, but finally he agreed.

Once that decision was made, Uncle Rudd replaced the lightbulb that had been shot out in the fixture over the workshop door. With the alleyway lit again, it didn't take us long to run upstairs and gather up our stuff.

The next task was to get Aaron's body into the bed of Freedom's truck. I volunteered to help Uncle Rudd and Freedom carry the body out to the truck. I figured they had enough to do digging the grave. Aunt Connie rummaged through her storage closet in the workroom and came up with two battery-powered lights. Freedom already had a spade in the back of his truck. Uncle Rudd had a shovel that he kept in the trunk of his car in case he got stuck somewhere in the wintertime. Aunt Nissa packed water jugs and food as her contribution. None of us had the heart to point out to her that food was probably not a necessary item.

We were just about ready to leave when Aunt Connie mumbled, "I forgot something," and went back into the workshop. She came out with a bouquet of long-stemmed red carnations wrapped in white tissue paper. Picking one flower out of the bunch, Aunt Connie handed it to Uncle Rudd. "I'm taking these flowers to Truman. They've got vases at the hospital I can put them in. But I'd like for you to take that carnation and lay it on Aaron's grave. I understand that we can't draw attention to the grave with a lot of flowers, but nobody will notice just one carnation. Hold it down with a rock or something."

Uncle Rudd nodded and gave her a hug. "I'll do it, Little Sis. You gals go on now. We'll be up at the hospital as soon as we can."

We left first, with me driving Uncle Rudd and Aunt Nissa's car.

When we passed Addison's Mill, none of us said a word. In the rearview mirror I could see Freedom's headlights. I watched until I saw them pull off toward the mill. I didn't say anything. I didn't see Aunt Connie turn her head or notice her looking into the passenger side mirror, but all the same, she knew, because I heard her sigh just as the headlights of Freedom's truck disappeared from behind us. I breathed a sigh of relief and drove on to the hospital.

CHAPTER SIXTEEN

We drove into the parking area where after-hours visitors could enter through the emergency room. When we pulled up and parked, Billy was outside waiting for us. He met us halfway.

"Hello, ladies." He smiled a tired smile and tipped his hat. "Been a long night, hasn't it? Otis called awhile ago and asked me if I'd stick around until you got here and make sure you got to see Truman. He's out like a light, but I've got it all set up for you to sit with him for a while if you want."

The three of us thanked Billy and gave him a hug. We could tell that he was tired and in need of being appreciated.

He beamed at us then looked around. "Where's Rudd and Freedom?"

"They had something to take care of, but they're right behind us," Aunt Nissa said.

"You don't have to stay, Billy. If you've already set it up so that we can see Truman, surely they'll let Rudd and Freedom in when they come."

Billy didn't look absolutely sure about that, but he was

evidently too tired to argue. "Yeah, you're probably right. I'll go in the emergency room with you, though, and let them know Rudd and Freedom are coming. Marsha Wallens is working up on the post-surgery ward where they have Truman. All we need to do is call her. She said she would come down and take you up there to his room. Marsha's brother, Sam Jeffcoat, is with Truman now."

"Why is Sam with Truman?" I asked. It was hard for me to imagine Sam and Truman in the same room together. They were such different people. Sam was quite a bit older, and in my opinion, wiser, than Truman. Sam's main occupation was cattle ranching, but he was also a lay preacher. The outstanding thing about Sam is that he is a man at peace with God and with life. I couldn't figure out what a sullen journalist like Truman had in common with someone like Sam Jeffcoat.

Billy shrugged his thin shoulders. "Sam and Truman have become pretty good buddies since Sam's wife died a year or so ago."

That certainly set my thoughts back a step or two. But I didn't have time to mull it over. Billy led the way through the emergency room to a phone in the hallway and dialed the three-digit number.

After he was done talking, he informed us that Marsha was on her way down to get us, and she would make sure they would send Uncle Rudd and Freedom up when they came through the emergency ward. Yawning, Billy added,

"Now that I know everything's taken care of, I think I'll just mosey on home. Got a big day tomorrow. Oh, that reminds me. Connie, Otis wondered if I could have the keys to the back of the flower shop so I could dust for prints and look for clues tomorrow. He said to just drop them by the station as soon as you could in the morning."

Bless Otis! He set it up so that if we didn't get Aaron's body out of the flower shop cooler tonight, we had time to do it in the morning.

"I always keep my keys on me, Billy," Aunt Connie told him as she fished them out of her purse. Taking one off the ring, she handed it to Billy. "I'll keep my apartment key and the key to the showroom. You won't need those. How long do you think you'll need to be in the workshop? We need to clean up the place."

"Shouldn't take more than a couple of hours." Billy shrugged and pocketed the key. "I'll be real quiet while I'm back there so's I don't disturb any customers. How's that?"

"That's fine, Billy," Connie said. "You go on home and get some rest now."

Billy took a couple of steps toward the door then turned around. "Uh, I haven't read the notes Otis took for the report yet or had much of a chance to talk with the sheriff, so I was sorta wondering if any of you saw anything or know why someone would shoot Truman in the back like that?"

Aunt Nissa shook her head. "We didn't see anyone."

Before Aunt Nissa could say any more, Aunt Connie

jumped in, and in a grumpy tone of voice said, "Seems like we weren't a lot of help to Otis."

Otis would have been very proud of my two aunts. After all, he told us that if anyone asked, we were to tell them that we hadn't been much help. Which, all things considered, was amazingly true!

Billy left just as Marsha came out of the elevator and greeted us. Marsha was an efficient woman. She had everyone in Emergency straightened out about Uncle Rudd and Freedom and ushered us up to the third floor in record time.

Warning us not to stay long, Marsha gave us Truman's room number then left to tend to another patient. We went down the hallway in single file to leave room for the nurses going back and forth. Since Aunt Connie was the one with the flowers tucked tightly in the crook of her arm, she insisted on leading.

At the doorway to Truman's room, Aunt Connie started to go in then stopped abruptly. Aunt Nissa plowed right into her and I plowed into Aunt Nissa. Aunt Connie whirled around and pushed us backward.

Raising a finger to her lips, she whispered, "Be real quiet. Sam's in there on his knees by the chair, praying."

Aunt Nissa rubbed her eyes. "Why don't we give Sam some time and go back down the hall to that vending area we passed and get us some coffee. I could use a little caffeine about now."

I didn't really want anything, so I told them I would wait

in the hallway for them.

Aunt Nissa reached up and kissed me on the forehead then followed Aunt Connie down the hall. I watched them until they disappeared into the vending area, then I peeked into Truman's room. No longer kneeling on the floor, Sam was slouching in the chair next to Truman's bed.

I walked just inside the doorway, and as softly as I could I asked, "How's he doing?"

Sam jerked his head up. "Dixie! Marsha told me you were coming, but I didn't hear you come in." He gave me a wide grin. "Thank the good Lord, he's doing quite well."

I noticed Sam's eyes were red-rimmed from crying, and he was sniffling to keep his nose from running. Reaching into my purse, I grabbed a tissue and handed it to him.

Ignoring the tissue, Sam got up and leaned against the wall a few feet away. "Guess you probably think it's kinda silly for a grown man to cry."

"I think it's silly that you go to the trouble to shed tears for a good friend and refuse to blow your nose afterward." I held the tissue out again.

This time Sam took it. Giving me a sheepish grin, he mumbled a thank-you and blew his nose.

I took a look at Truman. His breathing was even, and his color looked pretty good. I had some apologizing to do, but that could wait until he felt better. I hoped Truman would forgive me—for his sake, as well as mine.

"Sam," I said, "you look like you could use a little break.

There's a vending area down the hall. Aunt Nissa and Aunt Connie are down there now. How about we go get a cup of coffee or a soda?" I was hoping he would say yes. That way we could talk a little and not worry about disturbing Truman.

Sam agreed and we made our way down the hallway to the vending area. Aunt Connie and Aunt Nissa were just finishing their cups of coffee. They decided they would go on down to Truman's room and sit with him for a while. I could see that Sam was relieved that someone would be with Truman.

I got a soda, he chose coffee, and we settled down at a small round table. Purely as a conversation starter, I asked, "Did Marsha call you when they brought Truman in?"

Looking forlorn and bewildered, Sam answered, "Yeah, she knows Truman's a close friend, so she called me right away. You know, I talked to Truman on the phone earlier this evening. He was all excited about going over to the shop to have a meeting with you folks. Just never expected someone to shoot him like that. Didn't realize he would be in any danger. I should have seen it coming, though." Suddenly Sam grabbed his coffee, got up from his chair, and went to stand by the window. He stood there staring out at the black darkness. I got up and stood beside him.

Turning his face toward me and looking at me with sadness in his eyes, he said hoarsely, "I should have warned him or gone with him or done something!"

That didn't make sense. What could he have possibly

warned Truman about? "You couldn't have known what would happen to Truman tonight, Sam. None of us knew what was going to happen, except the person who shot him. It's not your fault. There's really nothing you could've done."

Sam said, "That's where you're wrong. Do you know why Truman was so excited about being invited over to interview you folks?"

I felt confused. As far as I knew we only told Truman he was invited over to talk about the burglary, and that's what I told Sam.

"That's not why he was excited." Sam slowly shook his head. "Truman thought he had a bigger story."

"A bigger story? What do you mean?"

Sam took my arm and led me back to the table where we had been sitting. "I don't know if I should be telling you all this, but right now I need to talk to someone."

He sipped his coffee and we sat quietly. I let him gather his thoughts. Finally he said, "Okay, here goes." Then he stopped and cocked his head slightly to the side as if he wanted to make sure he said the right thing in the right way. "Dixie, do you know much about Aaron Scott coming back into town?"

That was a question I hadn't expected. Now it was my turn to say the right thing in the right way. "I know he came back into town the other day after he disappeared forty years ago on the day he was to marry Aunt Connie."

Sam gave me a quick nod and watched my face very

carefully. "The thing is, a lot of people saw him in Kenna Springs, but nobody has seen him lately. According to Truman, nobody saw him leave town, either."

I could feel my heart pounding in my chest and my mouth went dry. I wondered just how much Truman actually knew about Aaron Scott. "So what does Truman think happened to Aaron?"

Looking at me from hangdog brown eyes, Sam only hesitated a second. "He thinks that someone murdered Aaron before he could leave town! Apparently he's done some checking and has sort of a theory going. He thinks that Aaron left town in the first place because of something he saw just before his wedding to Connie. Truman figures that whatever Aaron saw all those years ago got him murdered when he came back to Kenna Springs. Although Truman doesn't have a good answer as to why Aaron would risk coming back here in the first place."

I could have told Sam that Aaron Scott came back because a dying man has nothing to lose, but I didn't. Instead, I asked another question. "Does Truman have any idea what it was that Aaron saw the night before the wedding?"

"That's the thing. Truman felt pretty certain he had figured out what it was Aaron witnessed that night. He said that information gave him a pretty good idea who would want to murder Aaron after he showed up a few days ago. I figure whatever Truman knew, or thought he knew, is what got him shot. He wouldn't tell me the details. Truman just said he wanted to talk with all of you tonight and check a few things out. From what I gathered, he thought Rudd or Connie had some sort of information he wanted. I guess he wanted to go over what happened the day of the wedding." Sam finished off his coffee and crushed the now empty Styrofoam cup with his hand. "Truth is, I thought Truman was making a lot out of nothing when he told me he suspected Aaron Scott had been murdered. I figured Aaron just left town. That's all there was to it. But then somebody shot Truman!"

There was such anguish in Sam's voice I wanted to gather him up in my arms, protect him somehow, take away his pain, but I couldn't. We had promised Otis we wouldn't tell anyone. I could do one thing, though. I could point him in the right direction. "Sam, there was nothing you could have done to prevent this, but you can do something to help. You can call Otis and tell him what you know. Before you call, think about all the things Truman has told you about his suspicions. Try to remember every little scrap of information. Write it down. Make sure you tell the sheriff everything. And do it soon, Sam. Don't wait."

I saw a little hope come into Sam's eyes as I spoke to him. A thin, tight smile spread across his mouth. He nodded. "You're absolutely right. I should talk to Otis. I started to tell Billy, but I didn't. I kept thinking maybe there was some other reason Truman got shot, and I should just shut my mouth until I could think about all of this. I didn't want any of it to be true. But what other reason could there be?

Truman was on to something and it got him shot. Thanks, Dixie. You've helped me sort things out. You know, you listen well and ask good questions. You'd make a whiz-bang counselor."

Apparently Sam had forgotten that counseling is what I do for a living. That didn't matter at the moment, though.

"If you want to write down what Truman told you, I think I have a pen and notebook in my purse," I offered.

Sam shook his head. "I think I got it pretty straight. Although, come to think of it, I do remember something else Truman told me. When I asked him who he thought could have murdered Aaron, he wouldn't give me a name. The only thing he would say is that he needed to be sure because he was about to accuse a big fish in a little pond, and it wouldn't do to be wrong."

Sam stood up. "Listen, Dixie. I think while you ladies are here and can be with Truman, I'll go call Otis and tell him what I know. Besides, if Truman wakes up any time soon, it will thrill him that Connie came and even brought him some flowers."

I must have looked a little bewildered at the thought that Truman would be thrilled to see my aunt, because in a hurried fluster of words, Sam stammered, "Oh, dear. . . oh, dear me. That just flew out of my mouth. I probably shouldn't have said that about Connie. Please don't tell her that Truman has a crush on her."

"Truman has a crush on Aunt Connie?"

Sam's face flushed six or seven different shades of red as he explained. "Truman's had a crush on her ever since they worked together on the decorating committee last summer for the Kenna Springs Founder's Day Fish Fry. He's been trying to work up the courage to ask her out. So far all he's managed to do is to drive by her place every morning before he goes to work. You won't tell anyone, especially Connie, will you?"

All I could do was to stare at Sam and mutter, "No, of course not."

Sam left to go down the hallway and call Otis on the phone down at the nurses' desk. I knew I should leave also, and go see about Truman and my aunts, but I just sat at the table feeling stunned. I needed to sort out in my mind some of the things Sam had told me. I needed to concentrate specifically on what he told me about Truman's suspicions. But all I could think about was Truman Spencer having a crush on Aunt Connie.

I kept picturing Truman and Aunt Connie walking hand in hand down the street, while looking lovingly into each others' eyes. I physically shook my head to knock that picture out of my mind. Then I pictured them sitting in church together, sharing a hymnal. I had a hard time shaking that picture.

After a while I got used to the idea and decided it might not be a bad match. Although both of them had strong personalities and each of them had quirks, it might work. I wondered if Aunt Connie would go on a date with Truman if he ever got up the nerve to ask her out. I had to admit, though, that the picture of staid, rather pompous Truman attending a Tanner family reunion was hard to imagine. On the other hand, stranger things have happened.

It was almost fun, in an absurd sort of way, to think about Truman and Aunt Connie, but I needed to concentrate on Truman's suspicions. Purposely turning my thoughts away from the possible romance between Aunt Connie and Truman, I was finally able to concentrate on what Sam had told me. Praying for guidance, I began to focus on the last thing Sam had said about Truman telling him that the murderer was a big fish in a little pond.

I reasoned that if this big fish had killed Dolly, then it made sense that he killed her because he would have a lot to lose if she were alive. She had told Chad Gunther that some big shot was interested in her. Someone from Kenna Springs that she thought was going to marry her. It had to be someone not only from Kenna Springs, but also someone who attended the bachelor party. If not Truman, who would that leave? Who in Kenna Springs had the most to lose? Who could Dolly make trouble for, especially if he didn't want to, or maybe couldn't, marry her?

Only one name came to mind. Latham Sheffield. Suddenly I knew what Truman knew. It made so much sense. Uncle Rudd had said that Latham was engaged to Barbara at the time. Barbara's family was as well-off as the Sheffield family. Latham wouldn't want anything or anyone to prevent his marriage to Barbara. It wasn't hard to imagine that Dolly had interpreted his attention as love. It wouldn't be the first time something like that had happened. It made my stomach queasy to think that Dolly was murdered to save the Sheffield name and status. But how did Aaron Scott fit into all of this?

Whatever went on that night, Aaron was so scared he ran. I wondered what would have happened if he hadn't run, if he had gone to the sheriff with what he knew. Things might have been different. But he hadn't. He'd just left town and disappeared. Maybe he figured Latham was too powerful, and there wouldn't be any use in trying to fight him.

It was not just my stomach that felt queasy, my heart and my mind felt sick, also. Laying my head down on the table in front of me, I prayed. I prayed that God would protect my family, protect Freedom, protect Truman, and protect me. And I prayed for Latham, poor sick Latham. Not that he would get away with murder; no, never that. I prayed that Latham would somehow, someway, be stopped from harming anyone else. Maybe he would come to the end of himself and seek God's forgiveness.

Afterward, I just lay there with my eyes closed and my head cradled in my arms on top of the table. I really didn't want to think anymore or even to feel anything at the moment. I knew I had to call Otis. I had to tell him about Latham. I didn't know if he would believe me or not. My credibility with the sheriff of Kenna Springs was probably at an all-time low.

I reached into my purse and grabbed my cell phone. Flipping it open, I realized it needed recharging. I had just thrown it back into my purse when Aunt Connie and Aunt Nissa came whizzing through the open doorway of the vending area.

"How's Truman?" I asked

"Oh, he's doing just fine." Aunt Nissa waved a dismissive hand. "He woke up while we were with him. Sam's with him now."

"I'll say he's doing just fine! That drugged-up varmint woke up and asked me if I'd give him a little smooch," Aunt Connie said. "I told him I'd give him a fat lip if he kept talking like that."

"Oh, Connie, will you just let it go! I've already told you, Truman couldn't help it, he doesn't know what he's saying." Aunt Nissa frowned. "Anyway, it's not Truman I'm concerned about right now. It's Rudd and Freedom I'm worried about. They aren't here yet, and they've had plenty of time to do you-know-what with you-know-who. I think something is wrong, and we need to go find them."

Glancing at the clock on the wall, I realized that Aunt Nissa was right. They should have been here by now. Maybe they had trouble starting Freedom's truck or got it stuck in the mud somewhere. It was probably nothing serious, but maybe they could use a little help.

Looking at Aunt Nissa's face and seeing the fear in her eyes convinced me that my phone call to Otis could wait until morning. Relief visibly flooded through Aunt Nissa when I told her we would go and look for Uncle Rudd and Freedom.

Immediately, she took off through the doorway toward the elevators, leaving Aunt Connie and me to follow as best we could. Halfway to the elevators Aunt Connie poked me in the arm and said in a low voice, "That little toad Truman even made kissy noises at me." Then she screwed her lips up like a fish and made quite a few kissy noises herself. I managed to keep a straight face as we headed into the elevator. At the pace Aunt Nissa set, it didn't take us long to make it through the emergency room, out to the parking lot, and into the car.

Once we were on the two-lane highway, Aunt Nissa actually encouraged me to speed. Having a natural lead foot, I obliged.

Just a few miles outside of Brogan's Ferry it started to sprinkle. By the time we crossed the bridge and got to the turnoff to Addison's Mill, the rain was coming down hard and fast. I had to drive slowly down the dirt road that led up to the mill.

"We'll never see Freedom's truck or them, for that matter, in this terrible downpour," Aunt Nissa said anxiously.

There was no way to get directly to the entrance of the mill by car. Years ago, when the mill was thriving, someone had made a pathway to the mill through the woods from the road using flattened stones placed here and there in a haphazard sort of way. Since that was the only way to get to the mill from the road we would have to walk that well-worn stone pathway. Aunt Nissa grabbed a flashlight out of the glove compartment, and we got out of the car to make our way toward the mill.

The pathway wasn't very long, maybe no more than a hundred yards, but the rain made the stones slippery and the going slow. Because of the downpour, we had to walk with our heads down, holding on to each other's hands.

In between peals of thunder I heard Aunt Connie mutter, "Whoever murdered Aaron won't have to hunt us down to kill us. We'll all die of pneumonia."

Her crack about Aaron's murderer hunting us down reminded me that I hadn't told either one of them about Latham Sheffield. I decided I would wait until all five of us were together to break the news to them.

We came out into the clearing by the front entrance. We didn't see Freedom's truck anywhere.

Pointing upward, Aunt Nissa said, "Look, I think I see a light on the second floor. They're probably taking shelter from the rain in the mill. Let's go on inside and see if we can find them."

We could see the spot she was talking about. There was a soft glow shining from a huge hole in the second-story wall of the old mill.

Aunt Connie and I followed Aunt Nissa through the front entrance. The mill was old and rickety, but it did provide shelter from the downpour. I briefly wondered why Uncle Rudd and Freedom didn't just stay inside the front entrance, considering how the stairway boards under my feet creaked and bent as I followed Aunt Nissa to the second landing.

The smell of decaying wood was so strong I kept my hand over my mouth and nose. Behind me, Aunt Connie sneezed several times.

Several times Aunt Nissa called out Uncle Rudd's name, then Freedom's, but there was no answer. I could hear the anxiety in Aunt Nissa's voice. I didn't know what to say to make her feel any better.

Apparently Aunt Connie did know what to say, because she passed me on the stairs, which was no easy feat, considering the slim width and precariousness of the steps, to get close to Aunt Nissa. Tugging at Aunt Nissa's wet coat, she yelled, "Nissa, no use yellin' for 'em, they can't hear you in this storm."

Aunt Nissa nodded, and we climbed the last ten or so steps to the second floor in silence. We could barely see as we stepped on the floor from the stairs. The battery-powered light was placed on the other side of the huge second floor, giving off sort of an eerie, smoky light. Several feet away from the light, Freedom was sitting on the floor with Uncle Rudd's head cradled in his lap. As soon as Freedom saw us, he started frantically waving and yelling, "Go back. All of you get out of here. Run. Now!"

But it was too late. Latham Sheffield stepped out of the shadows with a gun in his hand. All three of us stood still, frozen.

CHAPTER SEVENTEEN

In disbelief, Aunt Nissa asked, "Latham, what are you doing here?"

"He's here because he killed Aaron and Dolly and tried to shoot Truman. I imagine he has the same thing in mind for us." I edged slowly toward Aunt Nissa and Aunt Connie, closing the gap between us.

"Well, well, Dixie, you finally figured it out, did you?" Latham's tone of voice sent a shiver down my back. "It was a good thing I kept an eye on you folks. It was right nice of old Rudd and his buddy here to bring Aaron's body out to the mill. And now that you ladies have shown up. . .well, I can't tell you how much easier that makes things. There is one thing I would like to know. Where did you put Aaron's body all this time? I've had a few sleepless nights over that, I can tell you." Latham reared his head back and laughed. It was a chilling, almost hysterical laugh.

His voice weak and breathless, Uncle Rudd ordered, "Don't tell that polecat nothin'."

"Rudd honey, are you okay?" Aunt Nissa started toward him.

Freedom waved her back. "Nissa, don't come any closer! Stay right where you are. There's a hole in the floor between us."

Aunt Nissa stopped moving. Without taking her eyes off Uncle Rudd and Freedom, she announced, "All right, I'll stay put. But something is wrong with Rudd. Tell me what's wrong!"

Moving a few feet forward, Latham said, "Let's just say that Rudd is in the shape he's in because he needed a little convincing." Then with his free hand, he turned on the second battery-powered flashlight. "Here, ladies, let me shed some light on your little problem."

Latham had both lights sitting on a wooden barrel near Uncle Rudd and Freedom. We could see that they were sitting on a portion of floor that came out about five feet from the wall, and looked like it was about six feet wide. There was no floor whatsoever on three sides. Latham had them sitting on what was virtually a ledge.

Since it was too far to jump from the floor to the ledge, I wondered how Latham managed to get them on it until I noticed that on our side of the ledge were two board planks. Latham must have forced them over at gunpoint then removed the boards.

Aunt Nissa moved quickly to the edge of the gap between her and the men. It didn't take but one look and she wailed, "Rudd, oh Rudd, you're bleeding!"

Moving up right behind her, I took a good look myself.

Fresh blood covered the side of Uncle Rudd's head.

"I'm all right, Nissa. The skunk shot me but just grazed my head. It looks a lot worse than it is."

Turning to Latham, Aunt Nissa balled up her fists. "He needs my help. You tell me how I can get to him this instant!"

Latham started laughing that hysterical laugh again. It was unnerving. Then in a cold voice, he said very slowly, "You ladies really don't get it, do you? Maybe if I spell it out in plain English, it will help. When I leave here not one of you is going to be left alive, so you don't need to be too concerned about Rudd's head."

I tried to reason with Latham. "I think the gun in your hand makes it clear what you intend to do. But what harm can there be in letting Aunt Nissa go to Uncle Rudd or letting them come back over to us?"

Latham gave me a curt nod, did a little half-bow. "Point well taken. What harm is there? Let's see. . .I could force you all on the ledge in hopes that it will just fall to the ground under your weight. Then it would look like a terrible and tragic accident. But that really wouldn't do at all, because one or more of you just might live, and I can't have that, now, can I? That would be like tempting fate. However, if all of you come over on this side, my problem would be that you might think that together you could overpower me. You see, Dixie, I know what you're trying to do. But you really aren't as smart as you think you are."

Actually, I wasn't nearly as smart as Latham gave me credit for. It didn't occur to me that if we were all on the same side, literally, we could jump him.

A slow, nasty grin spread across his face. "However, as a businessman, I have to take a few calculated risks. You see, I have a particular place in mind for your, shall we say, eternal resting place. A place that has served me well in the past. To accomplish that, I do happen to need you all together. That's why I didn't kill Rudd and what's-his-name before you got here. Not that I wasn't tempted."

Taking a few steps backward, he motioned with his gun. "Connie, you move over by Nissa at the edge of that rather large hole in the floor."

Aunt Connie moved over by Aunt Nissa and the two of them wrapped their arms around each other.

"Very good, ladies. Now, Dixie, you go over there and move those planks so that Rudd and buddy boy can cross over. But let me warn you that if any of you try any heroics, I'll shoot Nissa and Connie first. Understand?"

I nodded and made my way over to the planks. They were heavier than I had anticipated. After a good deal of pulling and shoving, I finally got them in place. When I started to cross over to help Freedom with Uncle Rudd, Latham yelled, "Halt, Dixie! Buddy boy helped Rudd over, he can help him back." Then he told me to go over and stand by my aunts. I did as I was told.

We watched Freedom help Uncle Rudd up. Uncle Rudd

looked unsteady on his feet, but Freedom stood behind him and held him up by placing his hands underneath Uncle Rudd's armpits. They started across.

I heard Aunt Connie gasp. Aunt Nissa grabbed my hand and squeezed it. I heard her whisper, "Merciful Jesus, please help them."

Slowly, they walked on the bending planks. Once Uncle Rudd stumbled, but Freedom kept his grip on him. Stepping off the planks, Freedom moved to Uncle Rudd's side, and they made their way over to stand beside the three of us.

Aunt Nissa went immediately to Uncle Rudd. After a quick look and a loving brush across his forehead, she turned to Aunt Connie. "If it's clean, give me one of those handkerchiefs you always carry around in your purse."

Aunt Connie opened her purse and produced a large white handkerchief. Handing it to Aunt Nissa, she asked, "How bad is it?"

Freedom answered, "The bullet just grazed the side of his head. We need to get him to the hospital as soon as possible, though. He's lost a lot of blood and probably has a concussion."

"Take Rudd to the hospital! Now that's funny, really funny," Latham said, only this time he wasn't laughing that awful hysterical laugh of his. "You people aren't paying a bit of attention."

Freedom leaned close to me, keeping his voice soft. "The longer we can keep him talking, the better our chances."

He was right! But before I could even begin to search my mind for something to say, Aunt Connie stepped away from us and moved toward Latham.

With a defiant look in her eyes, and as thunder pealed in the night sky, she yelled, "Why don't you just go ahead and get it over with Latham Sheffield! Come on, you murdering little coward, if you think you have to kill us, then do it! Heaven's a waitin' on us, Latham! Go ahead, send us to our Maker!"

I don't know how the rest of them reacted, but at the rate my heart was pounding, I didn't think Latham would have to use a bullet to kill me. Aunt Connie was going to accomplish that before he could.

Once she finished taunting Latham, she started toward him, screaming as loud as she had it in her to scream!

"Shut up, you old hag, shut up!" Latham yelled back.

I didn't like the look in his eyes. It was a crazy look, wild and darting. Suddenly, Latham picked up a gallon water jug that Aunt Nissa had fixed for Uncle Rudd and Freedom earlier and threw it at Aunt Connie.

It hit her in the chest. She lay on the ground fighting for breath. I got to her first. Bending down, I took her into my arms and held her up, praying for her to catch her breath.

Huffing and puffing, she looked up at me and then looked at each of us in turn with a disgusted look on her face. Finally, she managed to whisper, "You ninnies, you shoulda jumped him!"

I hugged her to me. This dear little aunt of mine had been willing to sacrifice her own life in hopes that while that madman was shooting at her, we would be able to get to him and save ourselves.

Feeling so grateful she was still alive, I wrapped my arms around her and hugged her tighter, until I heard her mumble, "Back off, Dixie June, it's hard enough to catch my breath."

I released my brave, but cranky aunt immediately. Freedom took over and helped her to her feet. As we stood there huddled together, I remembered what Freedom had said about keeping Latham talking. If Aunt Connie could be brave, then I could be brave, also. I decided to do what I do best. And that is to question and listen.

Struggling to keep the panic out of my voice, I asked Latham, "My guess is you buried Dolly somewhere around here, and since no one has found her you think that no one will find us?"

Another nasty, loathsome grin spread across Latham's face as he commented, "That's about the size of it. I'll give you village idiots a few minutes to make your peace, and then we'll take a little walk. I have some other business to take care of tonight."

Other business? The thought flashed through my mind that Latham intended to go to the hospital and find some way to do away with Truman, also. Truman had tipped his hand about his suspicions to Latham somehow. Otherwise, he wouldn't have tried to shoot Truman at the flower shop.

Surely he didn't think he could get away with so much killing. Nevertheless, my mouth went dry fearing for Truman. I hoped that Latham didn't know about Sam. Maybe Otis could figure it out with what Sam told him. But it would be too late for us, and maybe too late for Truman.

With frightening clarity, I knew that Latham had reached a point where he liked killing. It made him feel powerful and in control. Yes, he liked it enough not to want it over with too quickly. That was the only reason we were still alive.

In another flash of insight, I thought maybe I could use that against him. And in that moment, I knew what I was going to do.

After killing Dolly, Latham had forced himself to keep silent. Only one other person, Aaron Scott, knew what he had done, and Aaron ran away. With him still alive and out there somewhere, Latham felt threatened. He thought killing Dolly would end his troubles, but it hadn't. All these years he had secretly thought about it, had been fearful about it, had obsessed over it. For over four decades, Latham Sheffield had only himself to talk to about killing Dolly and losing Aaron. And it ate at him—consumed him. I was staking all our lives on the guess that Latham wanted to tell someone, talk about it, release all those thoughts, and I was going to give him the opening he wanted and needed.

Pronouncing every word very clearly, very slowly, I said, "Has killing become so easy for you? Do you think you can kill anyone, however you want, just because you're Latham

Sheffield? Was it that way when you killed Dolly?"

"You don't have the right to judge me, Dixie Tanner! Not you, not anybody." Latham's voice was vicious. "I'm only doing what I have to do to survive."

Glancing over at Freedom, I saw him nod slightly. His eyes told me to go on. I looked at each of my family, and each in turn silently told me the same thing. Encouraged, I stood a little straighter, pushed my shoulders back a little, and steeled myself, hoping he wouldn't pull the trigger on that gun. I was afraid of Latham. I wanted to live out my life, die peacefully, not violently. I desperately wanted all of us to live.

I prayed for guidance. I had to stay calm, alert. I didn't want to push him too far. I've always been fairly good at reading faces, watching for unspoken cues, so I focused on Latham's face. I told myself to watch carefully, then said gently, "I'm not trying to judge you, Latham. But if I'm going to die, I want to know what it is we are dying for. You had it all. Money, status, looks. You started all this killing with Dolly. What hold did she have on you? What power did she have over you, Latham? Did you love her too much or too little?"

I saw it! I glimpsed relief on Latham's face. It was just a flicker, but I saw it. He was going to speak the unspeakable things he had hidden away inside himself. In some ways, that flicker I saw on his face brought me hope, in other ways it brought dread. He was unstable, there was no telling, no surmising what he might do. But, we were still alive. So far!

"Love her! Love Dolly?" Latham's voice was high-pitched, almost hysterical. I didn't like the way his eyes looked. He was sweating, and it was cold in the mill. I didn't like this at all, but there was no way to stop it now.

"It wasn't about love, Dixie." Latham's darting eyes began to focus on me. "It was about having a good time. That's all! But Dolly didn't see it that way. She thought I was going to marry her. I tried to tell her I couldn't marry her. I told her I was already engaged and everybody expected me to marry Barbara. I didn't want to hurt her. I tried to break it off. I did!"

Latham wiped his forehead and chin with his free hand. His breathing was becoming rapid and shallow. The stress of telling the story was beginning to take a toll on him. I had to keep him talking. "But she wouldn't let you break it off, is that it? What did she do to you, Latham? Did she threaten you?"

Latham looked at me like he was seeing me for the first time. "Yes. . .yes, that's exactly what she did. She threatened me. I told her I didn't want to see her anymore. I thought it was over with. But she found me that night. Everyone had gone home after Aaron's bachelor party. I didn't want to go home, so I went out on the boat. Dolly knew I liked to spend the night on the boat, so she came there. She told me she wanted to make it big in Hollywood, and if I wasn't going to marry her, then the least I could do was to give her enough money to make that possible for her." Latham started laughing like it was the funniest thing he had ever heard himself say. He fell to his knees, but he kept the gun pointed at us. Finally he stopped laughing and started talking again. "Oh, that was funny, don't you think? Well, maybe you had to be there. I told her I couldn't give her any money. My parents had the money, I didn't. Not yet. She kept insisting, yelling at me, telling me I was nothing but a stupid rich boy. Then she said that if she didn't get the money she would ruin me. She would tell everyone about us. I couldn't have that! My parents would disinherit me if they knew about Dolly. If that happened, then Barbara's parents would make her break off our engagement. I would lose everything before I even had it."

Latham shook his head. His chest heaved, his mouth opened and closed as he gasped for breath. He started blinking rapidly, darting his eyes like he couldn't decide what to focus on, then he lifted his gun, and in a low menacing voice said, "I had to stop her. You see that, don't you?"

Latham looked about as much like the Grim Reaper as anyone I've ever seen. Cold, murderous, he stared at us for a moment. Then he changed. His body relaxed. He seemed calmer, more in control, like he had made a decision. I took that as a bad sign. Maybe I had pushed him too far. But there was no going back now. I had to keep him talking.

With a voice shaking as much as my body, I asked, "How did you kill her, Latham?"

He sounded dead, emotionless. "Kill her? I hit her just to make her stop yammering, and she fell overboard. I reached down to grab her hand and that's when I knew I could make her go away. I simply grabbed her by her hair and pushed her under. I held her that way until she quit struggling. That's when Aaron showed up." Latham started laughing again. "Stupid little man. Seems he felt bad about all the ribbing we gave him about not going on the boat. He knew I was still at the boat, so he worked up his courage and came out there to see if I would take him for a ride. Said something about not wanting Connie to marry a coward. He even tried to save Dolly's life. Did you know that, Connie? He thought it was an accident at first. But it didn't take him long to figure it out. We fought, but he got away. I hunted for him most of the night. While I was trying to find Aaron, I figured out where I could put Dolly's body. I brought her out here to Addison's Mill. I found a place inside the mill where no one would ever think to look."

Latham took a deep breath. "You know the rest of the story, don't you, Dixie?"

"I can put it together, yes. I think when you realized Aaron had come back, you knew he would go see Aunt Connie at the flower shop. All you had to do was watch and wait and call the sheriff when Aaron showed up. Then you followed Aaron inside, stabbed him, and got out of there, waiting for Otis to come. But then Dennis Reager had his little fender-bender and Otis never made it."

Latham's face turned purple with rage. "Morons! It was the perfect plan—it would have been over and done with right then if I wasn't surrounded by idiots."

I continued recounting my theory, praying I was buying us a chance.

"You must have been wild with frustration when, the next morning, it was business as usual in town. What happened to the body? And what about the murder weapon? Where was it? You broke into the flower shop that night, on a fruitless search for both. By the time you figured out that we weren't going to the sheriff, we had already moved the body a couple of times. You followed us earlier today, thinking we would lead you to Aaron; and instead, you discovered we knew a lot more than you thought we did. We knew enough to question Chad Gunther. That's when you tried to kill Freedom and me with the hay truck. And tonight you tried to kill Truman. Have I missed anything, Latham?"

Latham blinked a couple of times and his eyes narrowed. "I think you've just about covered it. Now you know why you are all going to die. So, now that that's done, all of you move closer to that great big hole in the wall to your left." Latham held the gun straight out with both hands.

Had we lost? Had we missed our chance? We moved in single file toward the hole in the wall. As I got closer I could see a broken-down, weathered grain bin near what used be a wall. Cobwebs were trailing in the breeze away from the gaping hole. It had quit raining and I could now hear the waterfall that once powered the mill's water wheel, splashing and crashing into the creek down below. Out beyond the hole stood the decaying water wheel, its massive gears pockmarked with rust for years. The millstone was gone, but the wooden chute that carried the grain to it was still partially intact. It hung inside the open wall by one rusty hinge.

As we huddled together by the hole in the wall near the water wheel, I decided to try one more time to talk to him. We had nothing else to try and nothing to lose. Taking a deep breath I plunged in, "Does Dolly still haunt your nightmares, Latham? Was there a time when you felt remorse at killing her? Do you feel any remorse at killing Aaron?"

Latham leveled the gun at my head. "Remorse is a luxury I can't afford, Dixie. I gave that up long ago. Now it is time for you to shut up."

I found that one can get reckless when one is about to die. I kept on, "Maybe you have managed to harden your heart so much that you feel no remorse. You might have even been able to keep killing Dolly a secret. But you've gone too far now, Latham. You can't keep on killing and expect to keep it hidden forever. You'll have all of us to think about now. We'll be in your nightmares, Latham. Yes, I think very soon now, it will all begin to unravel. You won't be able to stop it. You'll eventually make a mistake. You know you will. Put a stop to it now, Latham. Jesus can still heal the wounds in your heart if you will turn to Him. You are in a prison much worse than any judge or jury could send you to. Please,

Latham, before it's too late."

Latham took a step toward me. Both of his hands were shaking now. "I'm going to shoot you first, just so I can shut that stupid mouth of yours!"

Latham fired the gun! Someone shoved me hard, and I landed on the floor on my side. Feeling a sharp stabbing pain in my shoulder, I rolled over and saw that Aunt Connie was on the floor with me. Aunt Nissa was bending over us, trying to help us up. My thoughts were muddled, but I had enough sense to wonder why we weren't dead yet.

The answer to that question was less than ten feet away from us. While Latham was focused on me, Uncle Rudd and Freedom had jumped him. All three of them were on the floor struggling. We had a chance now, a good chance. But where was the gun? I didn't see it in Latham's hand. Surely if he had it he would have used it again by now.

I squinted my eyes looking for it. It had to be close. It had to be near the three of them. I saw that Latham was craning his neck. He was looking for the gun as well. Then I saw Latham grab something—not the gun, some piece of metal or a rock. He hit Uncle Rudd in the head with it. Uncle Rudd rolled off of Latham. His eyes were closed and he looked unconscious.

Now it was just the two of them fighting, each with purpose. While Freedom and Latham struggled, Aunt Nissa and Aunt Connie tended to Uncle Rudd. I got on my hands and knees to look for the gun. We had to keep that gun away from Latham. . . . And then I saw it.

So did Latham. It was only inches away from him. Freedom didn't seem to notice that Latham was trying to get to the gun. I lunged for it.

I couldn't grasp the gun, but I managed to kick it out of Latham's reach. Then I rolled over and scooted backward to get out of the way, but not before Latham kicked me in the head. The pain made me want to curl up in a little ball. I lay there leaning my head against the old grain chute and gave in to the pain.

Freedom and Latham were on their feet now. I watched through hazy eyes as Freedom tried to push Latham over the opening in the wall. They struggled and Latham turned, pushing Freedom to the edge. Freedom's arms flailed outward, then he fell into the water below. I heard myself scream and felt my heart break.

Latham started toward me. At first I thought he meant to throw me into the water, also, then I saw him turn toward my left and remembered the gun. He found it before I could even move.

As he pointed the gun at my head, his eyes were hypnotic and gleaming like the eyes of a wild animal. I froze, bracing myself for death. Then I heard Aunt Nissa scream my name, and without conscious thought I shoved the hanging grain chute toward Latham as hard as I could.

The motion of the chute stopped, and I heard a thudding sound. A coarse grunting noise came out of Latham's mouth.

He stood there, weaving back and forth, before he fell over the side and into the water.

I stared at the empty space where Latham had been standing. I stared, knowing that a second later I would've been dead. Then my mind went blank.

I woke up in Aunt Nissa's arms, her wet cheek against mine. Her voice shaking, she murmured over and over, "It's all over with, honey. It's all over."

My mouth felt dry. I tried to form words, but they seemed to crumble before I could get them out. I wanted to move, to flex my arms, make sure I was really alive, but movement was painful. Finally my mind cleared, and although movement made me wince, I managed to stand up with Aunt Nissa's help. As if of one mind, we leaned over the edge and looked out into the darkness below.

I didn't think anyone could fall from the second story and live. I felt little compassion or pity for Latham. Maybe that would come later. I hoped so. But sadness washed over me for Freedom. When the light of day came, would we find his body, broken and lifeless, on the jagged rocks along the creek? Would Latham's body be there beside Freedom's? One consumed with madness and evil, the other a child of God at rest in heaven.

Behind me I heard Uncle Rudd groan. Aunt Nissa patted my arm and whispered, "Rudd's coming to, I'd better see to him."

I started to follow her, but she took hold of my arm

and led me back to where we had been standing. Quickly, she retrieved one of the two large flashlights that were still shining where Latham had placed them. Handing me the flashlight and gently pushing me down, she said, “Hold this light up, Dixie, so that Freedom can see it and make his way back to us.”

Tears stung my eyes as I sat down with my legs hanging over the edge. I didn’t have much hope, but I prayed as I swung the flashlight back and forth, like a beacon in the night. I sat there, waiting, listening, looking.

Then I saw him! Shadowy at first, but it was Freedom. He was limping, but he waved at me and I waved back.

Elated, I called back to my aunts, still huddled around Uncle Rudd, and told them that Freedom was alive. Then I called out to Freedom that I was coming down to meet him at the entrance of the mill.

As I sprinted past Uncle Rudd I heard him ask, “What happened?”

Aunt Nissa answered, “The good guys won!”

EPILOGUE

After an overnight stay in the hospital for a mild concussion, Uncle Rudd pronounced himself, "Feeling well enough to be a burden to society again," and checked out of the hospital against doctor's orders.

Otis and Billy found the remains of Dolly O'Connell's body tucked in a fetal position in the backwash behind the waterfall that fed into the creek. The newspapers and television news crews reported that Aaron Scott's body was found near Dolly's remains.

A search and rescue team retrieved Latham Sheffield's battered body out of the creek nearly a quarter-mile from the mill. For what it's worth, the autopsy confirmed that the blow from the chute hadn't killed him. Latham Sheffield drowned.

In the week that followed, Truman Spencer rallied from his gunshot wound at a remarkable pace. By the time he left the hospital, he and Aunt Connie had a date to go to the Harvest Dance together at the end of the month. Miracles do happen!

I spent three days in the hospital. After I was released, Aunt Nissa had her hands full nursing Uncle Rudd and me. We loved every minute of it. She needs a vacation.

Freedom spent nearly a week in the hospital for a broken arm, two broken ribs, a mild concussion, and a sprained ankle, along with bruises and cuts. Aunt Connie nursed Freedom after he was released from the hospital. Now he needs a vacation.

As soon as the coroner released the body of Aaron Scott, we buried him in the family cemetery up on the hillside we have always called High Lonesome. This time he had a proper burial.

My parents have accepted Aunt Connie's offer to run the marina in Fort Walton Beach, Florida. Peggy is buying the flower shop, and Aunt Connie is buying the house next to Otis and Martha Beecher. Otis seems to like the idea. That way he can keep an eye on her. She feels the same way about him.

Freedom Crane and me? Well, let's just say that I'm going back to Little Rock to put my townhouse up for sale, give my notice at the clinic, and take Estelle Biggs out for a steak dinner. I decided to take Aunt Connie up on her offer and move into the craftsman house at Willow Cove. What happens from there depends on whether Freedom Crane turns out to be Mr. Wrong or Mr. Close-Enough-For-Me!

Teri L. Dunnegan, was a mother first and a friend second. She was born July 25, 1949 and departed this earth on November 14, 2006 from cancer. Although the pain of losing her has dulled, the memories of her never will.

Growing up I always thought my family was crazy, dysfunctional, and just plain weird. It wasn't until I was older that I came to realize my family wasn't crazy or dysfunctional and "weird" was just another word for "creative memories." I didn't know the day Mom grounded my friend for being rude to his mother would become one of those memories. But that was my mom. (He didn't come out of his house for a week, by the way.)

She always had a presence about her. She could dispense justice with a shoe or make you laugh in the most hopeless of situations. She gave wisdom when we were clueless and gave comfort when the world offered none. She always made everyone feel loved and welcomed. She was an example of Christ on earth and was deeply loved.

—Teri's son, Patrick

You may correspond with the family
of this deceased author by writing:

The Dunnegan Family
Author Relations
PO Box 721
Uhrichsville, OH 44683